Broken Pieces

Kelly Moore

Cover design by Kennedy Kelly at Cover Crush Designs

Editing by Tami Rogers.

Paperback Format: Formatting Two Broke Authors Formatting

Ebook format: Two Broke Authors

Other Books by Kelly Moore

Broken Pieces Series in order.

Broken Pieces

Pieced Together

Piece by Piece

Pieces of Gray

Syn's Broken Journey

Other Books

Next August

This August

Seeing Sam

Taking Down Brooklyn – co-written with author KB Andrews

Chapter 1

"Sex, sex, sex, is that all you ever think about?" My roommate's high-pitched laughter brings my mind back to the here and now.

"What? Just because I'd like to leave my teeth marks in the pizza guy's ass doesn't mean I am having sex."

"No, Brogan, it doesn't, but you should be. Your mind is always in the gutter."

This is true. I can't deny that my thoughts had moved from his ass to his front. Damn it. Cadence knows me too well. We became immediate friends our first day of college. Eight years later, she's the only person, aside from my brother Zade, whom I trust. I would give my life for either one of them.

"Cady, don't you have anything better to do than harass me about my sex life?"

"Ha!" a snort of laughter escapes her lips. "Admittedly, you have no sex life, Brogan. That's why we are sitting at home on a Saturday night, eating pizza and watching a chick flick. Besides, I felt the need to protect the pizza boy's ass from your teeth."

"I love you dearly, Cady, but why are you spending a Saturday night with me rather than with your hot-to-trot boy toy?"

"Brogan!" she yells in an irritated tone. "He's my fiancé, not just some boy toy! I swear, sometimes I don't get you. What is it with you and your lack of belief in love? You are gorgeous, smart, funny, have a great job, mad skills, much less a body to die for. Everywhere we go, men drool all over you, and you could care less."

"Cady, men only love what they see. They don't see the real me. You know my shit, Cady. You know all my secrets. If you were a guy, once you got past my looks you would run too."

"Yes, Brogan. I know your shit, and I love you anyway. Probably because of your shit and who I know you are, just as anyone would if you would give them more than a minute."

"Love is not for me or is anything I ever want. I am glad you have Jon and that you will have your happily ever after. That is what you want and need, Cady. Not me. My only love comes from a pair of double-A batteries."

Cady spews Coke across the room. I love embarrassing her. She's just so innocent when it comes to sex. Her sex life with Jon is plain old vanilla. Her cell phone rings, and she's running off to her room, giggling like a young girl in love.

My favorite movie, *The Notebook*, is on, but I'm not hearing any of it. I am lost in my own dark thoughts. Chills run down my spine, and I am suddenly cold, and I shudder at old ghosts.

Cady and I graduated with our bachelors in nursing at twenty-two. I continued on to be a nurse practitioner. At twenty-seven, we have both found jobs that we love. Cady works at a local hospital as a critical care nurse. I work in a plastic surgeons office three days a week in a nearby town.

We live in a small cottage on the bayside of the island of Redington, off Florida. It's a very small town, one way in and one way out other than in a boat, which is my preferred way to travel. My first purchase when I moved here was a 26 ft. Regal with a cabin. I would have lived on it, but Cady would call me a hermit and invade my small space. Cady and Jon are getting married at the beginning of next summer and moving to Jacksonville where Jon is interning to be a cardiologist. I will probably live on my boat at that time, but for now, I'm enjoying the roominess of our cottage

Cady cries every time she thinks about leaving me and begs me to go with them. I am happy here. It's peaceful. I have no fears, no worries, and I plan on keeping it that way. I will desperately miss her, but I will let her go.

The credits are now rolling; it's late. I peek in on Cady, and she is curled up sound asleep. I slip into my favorite sleeping shirt and swallow an Ambien. Every night, I tell myself this will be the last night I take one, but then a wave of terror runs through me, and I willingly gulp it down. Thank God, the effects kick in quickly. I hate being alone in the dark.

I wake up with a jolt. The clock reads 3:21a.m. I am soaking wet from head to toe. My only solace, thanks to my sleeping pill, is that I don't remember my nightmares. But I know there are demons behind my eyelids, and I shiver with the knowledge that I know what they are really about and from where they come.

I go ahead and get up. I know there will be no more sleep. I quietly slip on my running clothes and shoes, careful to not wake Cady. I grab my phone and earbuds, slip out the door, and crank up "Cruise" by Florida George Line, the remix version with Nelly.

One good thing about a small town is the safety you feel, and running this time of morning is beautiful. I run until I'm exhausted. I always stop on the beach until the sun is up. I breathe in the fresh air. It is so cathartic. Life has never been so simple, and I cherish it because I know one day everything will catch up with me, and it will all fall apart.

Chapter 2

My life is fairly routine. I work in the surgeon's office Monday, Tuesday, and Wednesday. I work out with a trainer four days a week. I love kickboxing and self-defense classes. Then on Thursday, I see the one person who helps me keep my ghosts at bay. I have been seeing Dr. Kohl for the past four years. His office is just across the harbor in your typical white-picket-fence office.

"Good morning, Ann."

"Good morning, Brogan. He's waiting for you."

Ann has been working for Dr. Kohl since the beginning of time. She's always mad at me because inevitable I am always late. Secretly, I think I'm late on purpose just to see her face crunch up like a prune in frustration.

Walking in, my mind floats to the song "Dark Side" by Kelly Clarkson. This should be my own personal anthem.

"I see you are your usual sarcastic self today, Ms. Milby," Dr. Kohl says as he winks at me.

"I wouldn't want to disappoint by being all nice and sweet." He smirks at me over his glasses. "Okay, okay, okay. What bullshit would you like to pluck from my brain today, Dr. Kohl?"

"Well, I don't know. There's just so much bullshit in that brain of yours, it's hard to know where to begin."

I can't help but laugh at him. I like him as far as shrinks go. "I would like you to figure out how I can sleep through one damn night without one fucking dream," I shout a little too loud.

"You're a little sweary today. Is there something else bothering you?"

"Why do you always have to act like such a shrink? Can't you just give a fucking answer without asking another question?" I am now shouting and pacing. What's more aggravating is that he just calmly sits there and smiles at me!

"It's my job," he says with a smirk and then points to the chair.

Okay, I can do this without yelling. I take in a deep breath and sit back down.

I take a moment to study him as he sips his coffee. He is attractive for an older man. I bet he was very handsome as a young man. I bet he was having a lot of sex when he was my age. "It's the lack of sleep…and lack of sex," I finally blurt out.

He chokes on his coffee, and the bastard just smiles at me. Damn, he has a pretty smile. Cady is right. I do have a one-track mind. Focus, focus.

"You do enjoy trying to startle me, don't you, Ms. Milby?"

"It's like shooting monkeys in a barrel, Dr. Kohl." We both laugh.

"Are you still taking your Ambien?"

"Yes. I just never seem to make it through the night without waking up in a sweat and yet chilled to the bone."

"Maybe you need to quit taking them so you can make it through your nightmares."

"We have had this conversation multiple times, Dr. Kohl. I am just not ready. Besides, I already know the ending, and so what's the point?"

"The point, Brogan, is to let your mind heal."

I say nothing. I just look down at my hands that are clasped together so tightly that my fingers are turning white.

"Would you like some coffee?"

He gets up and walks over to the coffee pot. He has made me coffee so often, he doesn't even have to ask how I like it. He really does know a lot about me, and I know so very little about him. Maybe I should turn the table and start asking him questions.

I am so lost in my thoughts, I didn't realize he is standing in front of me, handing me the coffee.

"What's going on in that head of yours today?" he says with his head tilted to one side. I think he genuinely cares about me. But instead of giving into his concern I respond with "How much I love caffeine," as I take a long sip of my coffee. He stares at me for a moment and then returns to his desk.

"Since you don't want to deal with your first issue of sleep, maybe we can deal with your next issue, which I believe was sex."

It's my turn to spew my coffee. "You know, Dr. Kohl. You really should think about your patient's safety before you just blurt out stuff. I could have burnt myself." We are both laughing again.

"Well, I am glad you avoided such an injury, but quit avoiding the question."

"I don't recall there being a question in that."

He draws a long deep breath in. I think he's frustrated with me. "The question was why is having sex a problem?"

"I'm not having any. That is the problem!" Great, now I'm back to raising my voice again.

"Why?"

"What? What do you mean why?"

"Ms. Milby, are we having another circle day? I ask a question, you ask a question, I ask again, and you use your usual avoidance tactics shit?" He never swears at me. He's definitely frustrated. Now he is clicking his pen. I need to give him something before that defenseless pen is broken in two. I sit straighter, unclasp my hands, and draw in much needed air.

"Okay. What was the question again? I will try not to pull my bullshit tactics," I said, mirroring back his words.

"Sex. Why is a young beautiful girl not having sex?"

I straighten again in my chair and try to lose the blush on my cheeks.

"Umm…I would love to be having sex, it's just that…I just like having it a certain way." I am now a deep crimson color.

"You have peaked my curiosity, Ms. Milby. Have you created a way to have sex that the rest of us are unaware of?"

I'm struggling here and the bastard is teasing me. Grrrr. "I, umm, I like…control and I, umm, like it rough." There I have said it.

I've told him one of my deepest secrets. I have just realized my eyes are closed. Do I dare open my eyes to see the horror on his face or is this where he tells me that I am just completely crazy. No wonder I am not having sex. I scare men away as soon as they figure it out at least that is what's happened in the past.

"Brogan. Brogan. Look at me." It is then that I realize I have been holding my breath, and I exhale loudly and gasp for air. "Brogan, open your eyes and look at me." He's moved. I can feel him in front of me. He's not touching me. He knows my boundaries, but he is very close. I peek open one eye, and yep, he is right in front of me, staring at me. Oh, this is serious. He's removed his glasses. I open my other eye and look into his. I think I see a hint of humor. Is he laughing at my proclamation? Surely not.

"Brogan," he says with a soft smile. "And you feel this is wrong?"

"Well, most men don't like a woman to be in control and wanting someone to be rough. Well, it scares them away." I close my eyes again. I just can't look at him. I can feel the heat on my face.

"Brogan, why do you feel the need for control and pain?"

I am suddenly up on my feet. I have humiliated myself enough for one day. "That, Dr. Kohl, is a question for another day." The reasons are just too dark.

Before I can make it to the door, he's standing in front of it with his arms crossed. "Ms. Milby, you have been seeing me for four years now. Are you ever going to trust me to help you? If you won't open up to me completely, how are you ever going to heal? I know bits and pieces that you have spoon-fed me. I learn more from your brother than you. And he's so loyal to you, he doesn't give much."

Just the mention of my broken brother brings up unshed tears. "How is Zade?" I utter softly.

"Worried about you. He wants to see you."

Zade is four years older than me. He is the only person that knows every detail of the horrors we lived through together. Zade had a breakdown when I went to visit him two years ago. It was too much for him. He has escaped to a little town in North Carolina, and thanks to Dr. Kohl, he is better.

"I, I can't. I can't risk him." A single tear rolls down my cheek.

"He is very strong now, Brogan."

Dr. Kohl travels once a month to see Zade. He took him under his wing the moment he met Zade, and he has treated him more like a son than a patient. I'm glad Zade has him, and the thought makes me soften toward him.

I smile. "Thanks to you, but I'm just not ready."

"When is the last time you went on a date?"

Whoa, change of subject. "I date. I just don't repeat date."

"I think it's time you try to have some sort of normal relationship with someone other than me and Cadence."

"There is nothing normal about me. Dr. Kohl, are you dumping me?"

"Never," he says with a grin. "You are far too entertaining for me to ever leave."

Somehow during our conversation, he has managed to have me sitting in front of him again. I don't remember sitting back down. "I am not normal, and I'm not lovable or worthy of anyone's love. I have nothing to offer back to anyone. You know how much I hate affection and emotions. Does that sound remotely like someone that has anything to give?"

"We have been over this many times. I see a bright, beautiful, self-reliant, strong, and sometimes bitterly sarcastic woman. What's not to love?" he asks with some humor in his eyes. I can't help but playfully pout about the bitter sarcastic remark, but I laugh. "We can work through your issues if you would just let me help you."

Help me? He is so sincere. He really thinks he can help me, and he hasn't even seen my dark side yet. Maybe I should unleash her on him. "You can't save me from myself," I say a little too harshly.

"Try me."

"Okay, you asked me about sex. How do I tell a guy I just want to tie him up, cause him a little pain, and fuck his brains out and then have him leave?"

Dr. Kohl opens his mouth to say something then shuts it. He repeats this process twice. Great! I've shocked my therapist!

He gathers his composure, "Well, it's not something I would lead with, and it's a bad pickup line." He's smiling. The bastard is laughing at me again!

I'm up on my feet. "That's all you got!" I'm yelling and pacing the floor again.

Dr. Kohl gets up and stands in front of me, but he doesn't try to comfort me.

"Look, Brogan," I know he only uses my name when he wants to get my attention. "We can work the whys of how you feel and change the way you think about yourself. I know some of your reasons through the little that you have shared with me about your childhood, but you have to trust me to get you to a healthy state."

I plop back into my chair, feeling a little overwhelmed by what I have shared today. He didn't kick me out and tell me I was a freak, so maybe I could try.

"I will try."

"Good. I want you to start that journal I have been nagging you about. Be completely honest. Nothing you write is going to chase me away. Shock me like you like to do, but not run me off."

We end our appointment with our usual handshake and nod. This is all my comfort zone ever allows although, today, I have an urge to hug him, but I stifle it. He seems to have read my thoughts because he smiles and says, "It's okay. We will get there. Just trust me."

Chapter 3

I'm tired and starving. I have forgotten to eat today, which is so not like me. I love food a little too much. I think it comes from starving in my childhood. We never knew when we would have food in our house, and even then, Zade and I had to share what little our father gave us. Thank God, I love to work out, or I would be as big as a house.

I dock my boat alongside our cottage. I can see Cady and Jon through the glass wall in the back of the cottage. Jon is here to take a much-needed week-long vacation. I see them have a tender moment and feel like I am spying. I wish I was capable of that kind of tenderness with a man. It would make my life a little less lonely.

I'm so happy for them. They met at the hospital during Jon's clinical rotations. Jon is a fourth year intern and will finish up next year. It was love at first for both of them. At least that's what they have both said. I'm so cynical. I don't believe in love at first sight. For that matter, I'm not sure I believe in love at all. I will agree that they have had a fairytale romance. Jon is always doing nice things for Cady. If he wasn't good to her, I would seriously have to hurt him.

Cady spots me through the window and comes running out and gives me a bear hug and almost knocks me over. This I allow from her even though she knows I hate it.

"I'm so going to miss you," she says. "I wish you were coming with us to St. Thomas."

"Cady, a threesome with the two of you will never work for me."

Cady smacks my arm. "You are terrible," she says, and she is instantly pink. Jon is walking up behind her, howling in laughter. She turns into his arms. "You, mister, don't encourage her filthy mind."

Jon tries to be serious with a shit-eating grin on his face. “Seriously, Brogan, I will miss you and your taunting of Cady, but you are not invited to come along on our vanilla weekend as you call it.” Cady is red from the neck up.

“You two are incorrigible,” she says, laughing.

“You two go before you miss your plane.”

“Will you be okay?” Cady asks quietly.

“I’m fine. If I have any problems, there is always good ole Dr. Kohl. You know I can take care of myself.”

“I know.” Cady sniffles. “I just worry about you.”

“No worries. Go and have fun on your vanilla week.” She hugs me again and then they are off.

Chapter 4

It's Saturday, and there's an annual seafood festival down at a place called John's Pass. There are shops and restaurants overlooking the bay. White tents are scattered along the waterway. There are at least a hundred boats off the shoreline. There is a long wooden walk with a dock leading into the water that is set up with a dance floor and a band. Being a small town, most every face is familiar except for a few tourists.

"Nice night out, Mrs. Jones."

"Hi, sweetie. Do you want your usual mint Oreo cookie ice cream?"

"Yes, please, but make it a large," I reply with a huge grin.

"Do you ever order any other size?" she says with a laugh.

Mrs. Jones and her husband have owned the local creamery since the beginning of time. They are the cutest little couple. They are in their eighties and still hold hands, and he steals a kiss from her every time I see them together. He says it's his "sugar" that's kept them together all these years. Mrs. Jones still blushes every time he steals his kiss.

"Here you go, sweetie." She hands me an overflowing cup of ice cream. "Now get out on that dance floor. I know my Joey would love to dance with you like all the other men."

Joey is her grandson she has repeatedly set me up with. Nice guy, just too nice for me. We hooked up one night when I had a little too much to drink and feeling a little too lonely. He was trying to be so gentle and sweet, and I tried to take the lead, and it scared him off. We never talked about it, but he is always such a gentleman when he sees me.

The fall night is so beautiful and the seafood is to die for. I hear the band playing a Kenny Chesney song, "Pirate Flag." I always want to change the words to "pirate boy" and "island flag." I am staring out over the pass, lost in the music.

"Excuse me. Would you like to dance?"

I turn around to find the most beautiful pair of pale blue eyes I have ever seen. It takes my breath and evidently my voice away. I don't know this man, but I'm drawn to him like a magnet. He has touched something inside me that I am unfamiliar with. I'm fairly tall at 5'11", but he stands above me a good four inches. He has wavy jet-black hair that curls down his neck, and a body that looks rock hard in his jeans, tight wifebeater shirt and cowboy boots.

I come out of my daze when he places his hand gently on my elbow. I quickly pull away and frown up at him. He is still just standing in front of me, staring with a stupid grin on his face.

"What?" I say a little too harshly. His grin is replaced with confusion.

"Dance?"

Oh, I had been so distracted by him, I forgot that he even asked me to dance. "Um…no. I'm eating my ice cream" I said as the sweet drips down my hand. Jeeze, am I crazy? What a lame thing to say. He is the first man I have ever been drawn to, and I turn down his dance offer.

"I could lick it up for you," he says with a wickedly radiant smile.

I can't help but laugh. It sounds like something I would say. "I don't dance with strange men or let them lick my ice cream or even share my ice cream for that matter."

"Ky."

"What?" I asked, totally confused.

"Name." He is still just smiling at me.

"Oh, is that short for something? And do you only have a first name? A true gentleman would have formally introduced himself before he offered to lick my ice cream," I say, teasing him.

"Kyren, and it you want a last name, that deserves a lick of that ice cream that is melting all over your gorgeous hand," he says, laughing.

"I have already told you I don't share ice cream. It is way too personal."

"Do you have a name, or should I just call you ice cream girl."

My mind is going there. I just can't help it, but my only response is that "As long as it's not vanilla, I'm good with that."

Then I see a spark of color change in those pale blue eyes. His pupils dilate, and I take a sharp intake of much needed air. He is no vanilla. I am instantly wet. That has never happened.

"Brogan," I whisper.

"Brogan," he says in a raspy voice. It's not a question. It's like he is soaking it in. It is such a turn on.

"Okay, Brogan that doesn't like vanilla, can we dance now?"

He holds out his hand, and so unlike me, I take it and follow him to the dance floor. Thank God the band has changed to an upbeat song by Hinder. He can really move. He turns, and I get a glimpse of his ass in his nicely fitting blue jeans. Holy cow! He is hot, and I can't help but think about my conversation with Cady about leaving teeth marks in the pizza boy's ass. It makes me giggle. He is fuckin perfect. He catches me looking down at all his manly parts, and I can't help but blush.

"That is a purely heavenly sound," he says, smiling.

"Yeah, the band is awesome."

"Not the band, Brogan, your laughter. You have a great laugh." The way he says my name makes me wet again, damn it.

"Well, you have a great ass."

"Do I now?" He is smirking at me. Bastard.

I am now happy about my choice to wear a short, flowing skirt. Two can play at his game. I really start to move, shaking my ass purposely, making sure my skirt flips up every now and then, giving him a glimpse of my long, lean legs. Even though the music is playing loudly, he stands stock still, watching me. His eyes are now a dark shade of blue. They are consumed by the dilation of his pupils, like he is soaking me all in.

I continue to dance around him, bumping up against him with each turn. This is fun. Suddenly, as I turn behind him, he grabs my hands and spins me around and pins my hands behind my back. I am so turned on and breathing really hard. I think he is going to kiss me, but instead, he releases my hands and gently rubs his hand down my face to my shoulder.

My demons take over, and out of instinct, I pull away, and before I have even realized what I have done, I kneed him in the groin.

He tumbles to the ground in pain, and all I can do is lean over him and tell him how sorry I am. I am horrified and embarrassed by what I have done. Before he can even catch his breath from the pain, I am running away as fast as my heels will take me down the wooden dock. I hear mumbles as I run through the crowd. I think I hear Kyren call my name, but I keep running. I run until I make it home, slamming the door behind me.

I fall to my knees, letting tears flow freely. This is why I am alone. I have yet learned to control my demons. I lay on the floor for I don't know how long until there are no more tears. I am numb. Now that my demons have been reigned back in, I feel fucking stupid. I was playing his game. I knew I was turning him on, and what did I expect? He had no idea of my limits. I really do need to have a deeper conversation with Dr. Kohl.

I finally crawl off the floor and go into the kitchen and find a bottle of vodka and take it to my room. I wish Cady were here to tell me what I should do. I look into the mirror at my tear-stained face. I feel so shamed of myself for losing control. My only saving grace is that Kyren is not from around here, and I will never have to face him again. I wash my face and quickly down half the bottle of vodka and crawl into bed.

Her crying is getting louder. I hear him telling her to shut the fuck up. Zade is sound asleep on the other twin bed in our room. I whisper his name, but he doesn't answer. I sneak out of bed and tiptoe to the door. Through the slit, I can see him on top of her, and she's still crying.

"Mommy," I call out. And as soon as I do, the door swings open, and he pulls me into the living room. I can see Mommy's face is bloody, but she doesn't move to free me of his grip.

"Come with me, kitten," he says, almost purring. He leads me outside into the barn. I cry for Mommy, but she doesn't come. He sits me on his lap, and he speaks to me so gently and brushes away my face with such tenderness that I think everything is going to be okay. He hugs me and brushes his fingers through my hair. "Hush, kitten. Mommy is fine. I love you, kitten. I won't hurt you."

I want to believe him, but I'm still scared. "Okay, Daddy. Can I go see Mommy?"

"No, kitten. She needs her rest, and I want to spend time with you. I haven't seen you all day." The stench of his cologne is making me nauseated. He continues to hold me in his embrace. I attempt to wiggle free, and his grip slightly tightens, letting me know he is not going to release me. I can hear his words, calm and soothing in my ear, but I have tuned him out and don't know what he is saying.

"Daddy, please, I can't breathe," I beg him.

Suddenly, he stands with me in his arms. He walks over to one of the old empty stables and gently lays me on the ground. Before I can even get up, he is on top of me, tying me up with a rope. I am screaming for him to stop, but he continues until he has my wrists firmly tied together, and they are bleeding. His words remain gently as he checks to make sure I cannot get free. He slowly unbuttons my night clothes. I continue to scream but have no rescuer. He lifts off of me briefly and undoes his belt and then he is back on top of me. "Get off of me!" I am screaming.

I wake up screaming, trying to look around the room and figure out where I am. I am drenched in sweat. It's pitch black, and I try to focus. I am in my room. I quickly get up and run into the bathroom, just in time to throw up in the toilet. It's a dream. Just a goddamn dream, I tell myself I am safe, I assured myself as I continue to hurl. Breathe, just breathe, I tell myself. It's over. I am safe. My head is pounding, and I wince, remembering the vodka I inhaled. I didn't take my Ambien. That's why I remember my nightmare.

Chapter 5

It's a breezy fall day on Monday. I dress for work in my scrubs and leave for work. The water is choppy, but in a quick fifteen minutes, I'm docked and headed into the office. I am still numb. I spent the rest of my weekend curled up on the couch, missing Cady's presence. I haven't eaten since the seafood festival. I haven't been able to stomach anything. Before I go into the office, I head for the local grind for a cup of well-needed coffee and a muffin.

I make it to work with five minutes to spare. Dr. Perry is sitting in his office.

"Good morning, Brogan," he says as he sees me.

"Hi, Dr. Perry." Dr. Perry is very sweet and good with his patients, and he has been very easy to work with. He is fifty-seven and has been married to the same woman for thirty-five years. They have no children, and I have never asked why. I try never to get that personal.

"We have a busy schedule today. I need you to see our new clients today and give me your professional opinion, which you know I respect." Normally he sees all the new clients. "I need to get out of the office early today for a fundraiser."

"Flattery will get you anywhere," I say, smiling.

He winks back at me. "As I knew it would," he says with a chuckle.

The morning passes quickly with a few minor procedures and follow-ups.

Dr. Perry pokes his head into my office. "Do you want me to pick you up something for lunch while I am out?"

"That's sweet, but no, thank you. I think I will just work through lunch to get us caught up." The muffin I had earlier is still hanging pretty heavy in my stomach.

"Are you okay today? You usually inhale food," he said in genuine concern.

"I'm okay," I say with a fake smile. "Just focused on getting done today."

I pour myself another cup of coffee and then buzz the receptionist to tell her to send the new patient to my office in five minutes. I sit back at my desk to review what information I have on our new patient, but before I have even opened the file, my door flies open, and in walks Kyren. My mouth falls open, and my face flushes. What for fuck sake is he doing here?

He straightens his shoulders and saunters into the room. He is standing in front of my desk. I am still just staring at him with my mouth wide open, and even though I am thoroughly humiliated by what I did to him, I am sure there is drool running down my face at just the sight of him. I have literally felt my heart skip a beat.

"May I sit or should I protect my balls first?" he asks as he openly covers his man parts.

I wince and then finally exhale. I hadn't realized I had been holding my breath. "Yes," I manage to squeak out.

"Yes to which? The sitting or my balls?" He has a soft smile on his face, and those pale blues eyes are hesitant.

"I think your balls are safe from where you are standing, so please sit down. Why are you here?"

"I have an appointment with the doctor."

Oh, of course. Silly for me to think he was here to see me. "I'm sorry. He is tied up and asked me to see his new patients. I fully understand if you want to reschedule with him."

"Maybe I should. My balls would probably be safer," he says with a smirk. He's teasing me, I think.

"No no. It's okay. I can see you. I know we got off on the wrong foot—"

He interrupts. "I believe it was your right knee, not your foot," he mumbles.

I flush red again. I start over. "I am sincerely sorry…"—I glance at his folder—"Mr. Nolan. I behaved very badly, and I am truly sorry for my actions."

"Kyren. Mr. Nolan was my father."

Do I have the right to ask him about his father? I decide against it and ask the more professional question, "Why are you here to see Dr. Perry?"

"I have a few deep scars. I would like to see what he can do to get rid of them."

"Scars on a man are usually battle scars of honor, and they wear them proudly unless they mar your face, of which I see none."

He laughs, but it doesn't reach his pale blue eyes. "The site of the scars don't bother me"—he glances at the business cards on my desk—"Ms. Milby."

Oh, now he is formal with me. I guess I hit a nerve. Why does he seem to bring out the worst in me?

"It's how the scars got there that bother me," he says quietly.

"Oh, um, I understand," I say too quietly. "Well, let's go into one of the examining rooms and let me have a look."

I come around the desk and stand in the door way. He hesitates for a moment and then follows me into a small room.

"Where are these scars, Mr. Nolan?"

"On my back, Ms. Milby." He says my name almost sarcastically.

"Okay, well. I will step out for you to remove you shirt and put this gown on—" But before I have even finished, he has pulled his shirt off over his head and thrown it on the table. Holy fuck! My mouth goes dry. I can barely swallow. His chest and abs are beautifully sculpted. I bite my lip to keep from letting a moan escape.

His eyes glimmer. "Enjoying the view, Ms. Milby?"

Smug bastard. Then he turns, and I see two thick, really deep scars making an X across his back between his shoulder blades.

I blink back tears, knowing the horror he must have gone through to get these. And here I have been such a bitch to this beautiful man who obviously has demons like I do.

I raise my hand to touch them. "How?" I ask.

His posture changes and his head hung down. He sighs and simply says, "A bad time in my life, and I choose to move on." He slowly turns around and catches a tear falling from my eye. He gently reaches up, and I take a step back. He lowers his hand. "Don't cry for me, Brogan. It was a long time ago."

Now I feel ten times worse about what I did to him. He has obviously seen his share of pain.

"I am so, so sorry for the other night." I turn to try and hide my shame. "Unfortunately, we could only diminish the appearance of these scars. We cannot completely get rid of them."

"I know," he says softly.

"What? But I thought you…"

"I just wanted to see you again. I found out where you worked, and I knew my scars would be a good excuse."

"But why?" I can't imagine why he would want to see me again.

"Apparently, someone has hurt you badly, and I don't want to be on that list."

"But how did you …"

"The minute I grabbed your wrist, I felt your scars, so I let go as to not hurt you and show you gentleness. But obviously, that was a mistake. When I touched your face, I felt your rage."

"I'm sorry, Mr. Nolan, but this conversation has just left my comfort zone." I turn to leave the room.

"Let me make it up to you."

I turn back around to look into the most sincere eyes. “I kneed you in the gonads, and you want to make it up to me? I think you have it a little backward and you are a glutton for pain.”

“Evidently, I hurt you too by my he-man tactics.”

“He-man? You aren’t going to club me until I say yes, are you?”

He laughs this big beautiful laugh, throwing his head back in laughter. “No, Ms. Milby. No clubs or touching from me unless you beg me,” he says with a carnal look in his eyes.

Oh, this man is hot. “There will be no begging from me, Mr. Nolan,” I say with soft laughter. If he only knew the real me, I would love to make him beg me. The heat in the room has just gone up ten degrees.

“So when would you like to make it up to me?” I say, teasing him.

“So, that’s a yes?”

“Yes.”

“How does Friday work for you?”

I feel a slight tinge of disappointment run through me. I was hoping it would be much sooner, like tonight. “Friday works for me.” I try not to seem too eager.

“By the way, Mr. Nolan, how did you know where I worked?”

“I know a good many things Ms. Milby. Small town, not too hard to track you down.”

“I have one more question for you.”

“Inquisitive, aren’t you?”

“Why did you ask me to dance and why are you in Redington?”

“For a smart woman, you can’t count. That would be two questions.”

“Just answer the question,” I say, smirking at him.

“One, I was visiting my aunt who owns the ice cream shop, and two, I couldn’t resist you. I saw a beautiful redhead leaning on a dock, looking lost in thought. At one point, you turned, and I got a glimpse of your lavender eyes. I was mesmerized by you.”

I have to catch my breath at his words. “Well, at least you were looking at my eyes and not my breasts,” I say, laughing.

He steps closer. “I would be more than happy to stare at your breasts,” he says straight-faced and then glances down, and then a smile curves his lips and reaches his eyes. I turn shades of red under his glare. “I will pick you up Friday at your place at six. Dress casual.”

“Don’t you need my address?”

“No, Ms. Milby, I do not,” he says, smiling.

“Stalker,” I say with a grin on my face and then he leaves.

The rest of the work day is tedious but goes by quickly. I just can’t quit thinking about Kyren. I have never met anyone who peaks my interest like he does.

Chapter 6

The rest of the week flies by. I have had so much pent-up energy. I even knocked my kickboxing instructor on his ass. That never happens. On Thursday, I find myself rushing to make my appointment with Dr. Kohl.

"Why, Ms. Milby, what gives? You are never on time," Dr. Kohl says with a sarcastic tone.

"I don't have time for our usual witty banter today. We need to cut to the chase."

I have totally got his attention. He leans back in his chair and pushes his glasses up his nose. "Go on."

"Sex!" I say a little too loudly.

"Um…is that a question or a proposal?" he asks with a grin.

"No, it's going to be our topic of conversation."

"Would you like to sit down first?" He points to the chair.

I didn't realize I had been pacing from the moment I walked in the door. "No, I just want to keep moving while we talk," I say as a shiver runs down my spine. "You know the story of my father." It's a statement not a question.

"Yes, but not details from you, only from Zade, and he would never tell me things about you."

"He would tie my hands up with a thick rope so that I couldn't get away." I subconsciously rub my wrists. Tiny scars still remain. I hesitate.

"Go ahead, Brogan. You're safe with me."

"It was the only harshness I would feel. His words were always sweet and tender. He would tell me how beautiful I was and how much he loved me. No matter how much I fought against him and my restraints, his touch was always gentle once he had me bound." I let out a deep sigh.

"Keep going, Brogan," Dr. Kohl urges me.

"I would rather have him beat me or, better yet, kill me rather than have his gentle touch. My mom, he beat, but she gave up her struggle with him when she started drinking. Then one night, she just didn't stop drinking, and she never woke up. That's when he started attacking Zade. He had to have someone to beat. I just don't understand why it wasn't me."

"Brogan, I know Zade's issues. I want to hear more of yours."

"I can't stand for a man to speak or touch me gently. I like rough sex, but I don't want to be the one tied down. I want to be in total control. It's the only way I know, so I scare off men."

"Thus comes the 'tie them up and fuck them' comment."

"Exactly," I say with force behind it.

"You know your father was sick, right?"

"Of course, I do," I say frowning.

"Men can be gentle and loving and mean it. Some men like rough sex, but they usually want to be the one being rough and in control. And it is okay as long as it's consensual. What type of relationship are you working toward?"

"I'm not talking relationship. I can't let myself go there."

"For you to be talking to me about this, something has changed. Have you met someone?"

"Um…um…why?"

"As long as you have been seeing me, you have never been this forthcoming with information, so whoever he is, maybe there is more to it than sex."

I stop pacing in front of his desk. "Are you going to fix up my 'fucked upness' or not?" I asked through gritted teeth.

"Brogan, we can work on your issues, but you have to start being honest with yourself and start by facing your past head on."

I am still just standing in front of him, my arms are crossed, and I am glaring at him.

"Take it slow and easy with whomever it is you have met. One day at a time, one touch at a time, and don't overthink every word that comes out of his mouth. Above all, be honest with him. Tell him what you want and need."

"Let me get this straight. You want me to tell him that I want to tie him up and fuck him and maybe even cause him a little pain all while he shuts his mouth so pretty words don't spill out? That is a fucking brilliant plan, Dr. Kohl. You are a genius!"

"Brogan, calm down." He has come from behind his desk and is inches from me. "That is not what I meant. I want you to tell him what it is you need in a relationship, tell him of your past."

"Oh, even better plan. He will know 100 percent that I am fucked up and will never be capable of a relationship."

"Brogan, one day at a time. Let him get to know you first. Enjoy spending time with him. Build a relationship, and you might be surprised of the outcome."

I literally growl at him in frustration, "My hour is up." I turn to storm out.

"Brogan, just think about what I have said, and next week, I want you to tell me everything about what happened to you as a child."

"With the advice you gave me today, you will be lucky if I ever speak to you again." I make a dramatic exit by slamming the door. Childish, I know. Damn it. That didn't go at all like I wanted. I feel a little guilty about the way I treated him but not enough to go back in and face him.

Friday, I spend three hours kickboxing, getting my ass kicked out of me this time. I cannot concentrate. I am mulling over the things that Dr. Kohl said to me, and I am worried about my date with Kyren tonight. I can't wait for Cady to be home on Saturday. I have missed her and can't wait to fill her in. She is my voice of reason.

I head home and take a long, much-needed hot shower. I keep trying not to think about Kyren's muscular body. It's very distracting. I get out and wrap my hair and body in a towel. I wipe the heat from the mirror and look into my lavender eyes, eyes that I have always hated. I can't bear to look at myself in the mirror. Next task, what to wear? I go to my closet and chose a soft, flowing deep coral dress that ends just above my knees. It only has one shoulder strap on the left side. Sexy, I think, but simple. The corral brightens my eyes and looks striking with my long auburn hair. My hair is so unruly with its curls. I attempt to brush it out and end up putting it into a fishtail braid, draping it over my right shoulder. I choose a long silver fetti necklace, big silver hoop earrings, and a small diamond stud for my nose.

Next are my shoes, which is much more complicated due to the fact that I am not very graceful in heels. He did say casual, so I'm going with a pair of silver sandals that are flat. As I dress, I am repeating my new mantra given to me by dear old Dr. Kohl, "Slow and easy. Slow and easy."

I hear a knock at the door. I turn to look at the clock. It is exactly six. I walk slowly to the door, take a deep breath, and open it.

And there he stands. Oh. My. God, I said to myself. He is dressed in a white buttoned-down shirt and jeans that mold perfectly to his body and a pair of cowboy boots. I have said nothing. I can't even draw in a breath. I'm just staring.

"You look beautiful, Brogan," he says, scanning my body down and then up. I had yet to breathe until he said the word "beautiful." I tell myself, It's just a word. Slow and easy as I remember my mantra.

"May I come in?" he's asks hesitantly.

I open the door wider and move aside and gesture for him to come inside.

"Nice place," he says as he enters

The living room is all white with splashes of teal and black. It opens up onto a deck that overlooks the bay. We have an outdoor kitchen and a custom-built outdoor fireplace.

I can only watch as this gorgeous man stalks through my living room to the outdoor area.

"Wow! Nice view too."

The only thing I manage to squeak out is, "Perfect. Just perfect," except for the fact that my eyes have not left his ass. He turns and catches me.

"Admiring the view," he states.

I look up and catch his meaning. "The view is perfect," I state again, only this time more firmly and grinning from ear to ear.

"Yes, the view is perfect," he said, and in five long strides, he is standing in front of me. His gaze once again roam my body, and I am instantly wet. Damn him. He reaches out to touch my hand but stops midair.

"What?" I whisper.

"I want to know that my balls are safe if I touch you." His other hand has automatically covered his crotch.

I giggle. "Your balls are safe for now, Mr. Nolan."

He takes my hand and kisses it and gently rolls my hand over displaying my wrist. With his other hand he traces the fine scars that remain on my wrist. I move to take my hand away, and he stops me.

"You have seen mine and now I want to see yours. I want to see what keeps you at arm's length."

I find myself whispering, "They are better now. Dr. Perry does great work."

I gasp as he softly kisses my wrist. All I can think is, Slow and easy, slow and easy.

"Pl-Please don't." It's a plea. I try very hard not to yank my hand away from him.

He lets go. "I'm not going to hurt you Brogan." He is staring at me with sad blue eyes.

I don't want to see pity in his eyes, and instead of giving into his kindness, I snap back, "Damn right, you won't. I have come a long way from a helpless little girl to a woman who can kick ass. So if you know what's good for you, you can keep your hands to yourself mister."

Instead of getting angry, he is standing there grinning. "I really just want to get to know you, Brogan, if you will let me."

"Why?" I breathe out.

"I'm just drawn to you. I tried to get you out of my head after you unmanned me in front of a crowd, but you're in my head, and I need to be near you."

"You are scaring the fuck out of me, Kyren. You don't know me at all."

"Well, let's remedy that. Shall we go?"

"Yes," I finally breathe out. He has blown me away with the things he has just told me. I am scared shitless but curious.

He opens the door and I follow. He is driving a white Ford F250. Thank fuck I decided against heels. It will be hard enough to climb into it with my dress on and try to be ladylike.

He opens the door for me, "Would you like help up?" he asks with a shit-eating grin on his face.

"No, I am more than capable of getting into a truck," I say as I miss the step, slipping and falling against his hard body. He takes me and lifts me up, placing his hands on my ass. Bastard.

"I figure me balls are safe from you way down here," he says, looking up at me, grinning like he got away with something.

This time I really call him a bastard. He laughs and slams the door. I can't help but smile.

Our conversation is light as we travel to the mainland. I have yet to ask him where we are going. I have been too busy watching him as he speaks. He really is very handsome. I am lost in my dark thoughts when we pull up to a marina.

"We are here."

"Are we going by boat?" I say confused.

"Nope." He gives nothing away.

As we turn the last corner, there is a yacht sitting at the end of the dock. His face is beaming in excitement.

"Is it yours?" I am smiling like an idiot back at him.

"It's my home."

"You live on a yacht?"

"Yep, and I own the marina, and I build yachts. So now you know something about me," he says as he turns in his seat to look at me.

Before I can stop myself, I blurt out, "I want to know how you got the scars on your back."

"Do you now, Ms. Milby? I will tell you when you tell me about yours," he says in all seriousness.

"Not going to happen," I say quietly, thinking he can't hear me.

We stare at each other, neither one giving in. He finally breaks our silent staring. "Why don't we start with the easy stuff over dinner?" He opens his door and climbs out. He steps around to my side and opens the door, offering his hand. This time I take it, not wanting to make a fool of my graceful self.

Inside, the yacht is beautiful and very masculine, dark colors and straight lines. He leads me to the living area. "Make yourself at home. I will go tell the captain we are ready to go out for a bit."

"I thought we weren't going for a boat ride?"

"Oh, sweetheart, this is no boat. Trust me when I tell you there is no comparison," he says with a beautiful smirk on his face. Before I can even respond, he is gone. I can feel how comfortable and in control he is here. I like the confidence I see in him. It's very attractive.

A female voice interrupt's my thoughts of Kyren. "Would you like a glass of wine?" The voice is from an older stout-looking woman.

Kyren reenters the room from behind me. "This is Mrs. Moore. She is my cook."

"Oh, it is very nice to meet you, Mrs. Moore. I would love a glass of wine."

"Make it two glasses, Mrs. Moore. Thank you."

"Come. Mrs. Moore already has dinner on the table for us. I hope you like steamed oysters?"

"One of my favorites, Mr. Nolan." He doesn't offer his hand but leads me to the table that has been set for us out on one of the decks. He is such a gentleman. He pulls my chair out for me.

The table is covered with food. My mouth is watering at the sight of the oysters. "Dig in," Kyren says as he sits down.

We both immediately start digging out oysters as Mrs. Moore brings out a bottle of wine and presents it to Kyren. For such a casual guy, he seems very formal with her. "Perfect choice, Mrs. Moore." She smiles at him and fills our glasses.

"Thank you, Mrs. Moore." She nods at me and disappears.

I'm not ladylike in my efforts of eating oysters. In between bites, we have casual, normal conversation. Comfortable. Almost too comfortable.

Mrs. Moore slips in, quietly refilling our glasses and bringing out the main course. "It smells heavenly, Mrs. Moore." She looks very pleased, "it is salmon with lemons and thyme butter."

I take a quick bite. "Oh my god, you are a genius in the kitchen," I say as I wipe my mouth. She winks at me and disappears again.

Over our meal, Kyren tells me how he got started into building yachts and owning a marina. He tells it with such passion. I know he loves his work. I am soaking in every word. I am drawn to him, just like he has said he is to me.

"So you dropped out of a prestigious college, borrowed money from your uncle, and built your empire?"

"Well, it wasn't that simple. There were a lot of hard knocks on the way. But, yes, I have made it very successful. I always knew that I wanted to build boats. That desire just grew into really big boats," he says playfully. "I built my first boat at eight years old. It was built out of an old tree my father had chopped down for firewood. I was stealing pieces faster than he could cut it. I still have it. It's displayed in my office."

"How did your parents feel about you dropping out of school?"

"My parents died in a plane crash when I was twelve. My uncle raised me after that." He has stilled for the first time since our conversation started.

"I'm so sorry, Kyren."

He regains his composure. "Don't be. It was a long time ago, and my uncle loved me and did the best he could. He supported me every step of the way."

"Where is your uncle now?"

"Uncle Tom lives in the trailer at the other end of the marina."

"What? No yacht for him?" I ask teasingly.

"Ironically, he hates boats"

"Really," I say, laughing.

"Actually, it's more the water he hates than the boats. He won't even step foot in one unless it's on dry land."

"That is too funny."

Kyren sits back in his chair and crosses one ankle over a knee. He takes a deep breath in like he is going to tell me a secret. What he says next takes me by surprise.

"Okay, Ms. Milby, your turn."

"My turn for what?" I say as I sit back in my chair.

"I want you to tell me something about you."

"Okay. No more Ms. Milby, Mr. Nolan crap. Agree?"

"Agree," he says with a grin, and his eyes have suddenly turned a deep shade of blue.

I am suddenly turned on just by the slight change in his eyes. I squirm a little in my chair and clamp my legs together.

He slightly parts his lips and inhales. Bastard. He knows what he is doing to me. I straighten in my chair, trying to ignore the ache between my legs.

"I'm a nurse practitioner."

"Yes, I know that. This is not new information," he says, staring at me.

"I grew up in a small country town in Georgia. I went to Auburn University for my nursing degree. That's where I met my best friend and roommate, Cadence."

I remain quiet for a moment, hoping that will fulfill his need for information.

"Go on."

"That's it. Short and sweet."

"You don't give away much do you?"

"What do you want me to say?" He remains quiet and just stares at me. "My parents fucked me up," I blurt out with a little too much hostility. Now I'm embarrassed. What happened to slow and easy? Gah!

He leans forward on his elbows, "Thus the scars?"

"Look, I have had a great time until now. I really don't want to get into all my fucked upness on our first date." I lock my hands together and stare down at them. I can't believe what I just said to him. Why do I let him get under my skin so easily?

"First date. Does that mean there will be a second?" he asks, grinning.

I have just told this man, rather rudely, that I'm fucked up and he focuses on a second date? He may possibly be more fucked up than me. He looks normal. He obviously has money. He is beautiful and could have any woman in the world. It's the wine, or better yet, it's the oysters making him lose his mind. That's it! Alcohol and an aphrodisiac. It must be the combination of the two.

I must have been talking to myself too long because I hear, "earth to Brogan."

"You…you want a second date?" I say with my mouth hanging open.

"Yes, I would love a second date, but can we finish the first one, he says smiling a beautiful wide-toothed smile.

"You may possibly be more nuts than me. I knee you in the crotch the first time we met, I tell you how fucked up I am, and you want another date. You have lost your mind." I can't help but smile and laugh at him as I am ranting.

He sits back in his chair. His smile is now gone, and his eyes are the color of a storm. "I have told you I am drawn to you," he says with all seriousness.

I swallow hard. "What do I say to that, Kyren?"

"For now, just say I can see you again, and we can get on with the rest of our evening."

I can't help myself. I whisper, "Yes."

"Good. Now tell me all about your best friend and your job."

We talk for what seems like hours. I tell him all about Cady. That seems easy enough to do. Then I tell him about my boat, small in comparison to his, but he seems to be impressed that I can handle and maintain a boat.

"Girl after my own heart," he says, smiling.

I giggle.

"What a beautiful sound. Your eyes light up when you smile."

"I have always hated my eyes. They are such an odd color."

"They are very striking and different. Like you," he says as he is staring into my eyes. He takes my breath away.

He tells me about a new customer that he is in the process of building a yacht for. "It should be completed soon." He pulls out the blueprints to show me the layout. "The odd thing is the guy wanted a hidden room off the master bedroom. See," he points to it.

"Is he a drug smuggler?" I ask, wide-eyed

"I don't know. He's very private. Maybe," he says with a shrug. He looks lost in his thoughts. Then suddenly, he turns and offers me his hand. "Would you like to dance?"

"What? Here?"

"Out on the deck." Before I can answer, he takes my hand and leads me to the top deck. The night sky is beautiful and the air has a touch of fall. A soft crooning music is playing and white lights suddenly turn on around the railing. I catch him placing something in his pocket.

"Did you just turn the music and lights on by remote?" He says nothing but gives me a full on grin. "Very romantic. Do all your dates swoon over this?" I say, teasing him.

He steps very close to me but doesn't touch me, and his eyes are the color of a storm again. "I have never brought a woman here before." His look consumes me and I shudder a little.

"Oh!...Why me?"

"I've told you. I'm drawn to you." He takes a step back and holds out his hand. "I prefer to lead if that's okay with you," he says with a smirk on his face.

"Only on the dance floor." I hear him inhale and see his eyes dilate.

"You like to lead in other areas?" he says with a hint of a growl to his voice and sweeps me around to dance.

He and I dance well together, and I don't even mind that he has placed his on firmly on my ass. My nipples harden as he presses into me, and I can feel the bulge in his jeans. I am breathless not from dancing but from the heat that is between us.

"Yes," I manage to whisper out.

"Yes what?" His breath in my ear.

"I prefer to lead in other areas," I whisper back in his ear.

"Tell me what you want, Brogan."

My name on his lips only deepens the pool of heat in my belly. I lean in and nip his ear. "I want to fuck you."

We stop dancing. He makes this sexy-as-hell growling sound, "Here on the deck or in my room, your choice?"

"Your room," I say huskily. Truth be known, here and now would be fine with me. I can't wait to get my hands on him.

He inhales but doesn't say another word. He leads me down two levels to the back of the yacht. His room is massive. A large bed sits in the middle of the room. It's covered only in gray satin sheets. The lighting is soft, and the same music is playing in the background.

He unbuttons the top button on his shirt and turns toward me. "Normally, I am very domineering during sex, but you seem to need control. For now, I will allow it."

Allow it? Why is that such a turn on coming from him? I walk over to him, and still his hand that has continued to slowly unbutton his shirt. "I like control too, Kyren," and I continue to unbutton his shirt and untuck it. I stop and run my fingers through the patch of hair trailing downward. I pause to admire his six-pack abs. I unconsciously lick my lips.

"Now what, Brogan?" he says through clinched teeth.

"Take off your pants," I command.

In one swift move, he leans down, removes his boots, jeans, and boxers. His cock is beautiful and large. He smirks at me as I admire him.

"Like the view?"

"Very much so," I purr. I reach out and grab his cock. It is firm and throbbing. I hear his intake of breath. I look up and he is biting his lip to keep from moaning. It is sexy as hell. I stroke him roughly a few times.

"Sit on the edge of the bed and keep your hands at your sides. Do not touch me. He hesitates, but he does it.

I slip off my sandals and very slowly pull at them hem of my dress and pull it over my head. I am left wearing a gray bra and slim to nothing panties. His eyes dilate even more. They look black and his look is smoldering hot.

"Enjoying the view?" I ask, parroting his earlier question.

"Very much so."

I move closer to him, and he starts to lift his hand. I take a step back.

"I'm sorry. I forgot. I am just use to being in control and taking what I want. And I. Want. You," he says each word seductively. "You are beautiful."

A chill runs down my spine at his words. Fuck! Slow and easy. "If you speak again, I will gag you." It is the only way I can think of to keep him from offering his pretty words. I want this, and I don't want to stop.

"You don't like to be told you're beautiful, do you?"

I say nothing and I turn and open a door that I'm hoping is a closet. The lights come on when I open the door. It is huge. I stay focused and quickly find what I am looking for. I return to stand in front of him with a navy blue tie.

He gapes at me. "That is usually my tool of choice," he says with a soft sexy growl.

"Open your mouth." He hesitates but complies. I reach around him, lightly rubbing my breast purposely across his face, and I hear him moan deep in his throat. I have to squeeze my legs together to keep from coming.

"That has to be the sexiest sound I have ever heard," I whisper into his ear. I stand back to look at him. "That will have to do for now. He looks so damn sexy. I kneel in front of him and start stroking his cock. Dew has already formed on the tip. I lean down and draw him into my mouth. He nearly bucks off the bed.

"Sit still," I demand and continue to lick and suck him in. When I start to feel him shudder, I stop. He lets out another moan, and I lick my lips.

His eyes are completely black and light beads of sweat are forming on his skin. I slowly reach back and unfastened my bra and throw it to the side. He stares at my full, aching breasts and then skims his eyes to my tattoo that runs the length of my left side.

"Look at me," I command again, and his eyes immediately meet mine.

I shimmy out of my panties. I reach toward him and loosen the tie from his mouth. "No talking or I will gag you again. Understand?"

He says nothing. Instead, he shakes his head in response.

I get on my knees again, but this time, I kiss him hard. Our tongues are immediately entwined in passion. I am pulling at his hair when I feel him grab my waist as he turns me and throws me on the bed. He is on top of me and has me pinned with his hard body. He has not grabbed my wrists. Probably out of fear for his balls.

"What happened to no touching," I rasp out.

"I couldn't stand it a minute longer. I need to be inside you."

He is spreading my legs apart with his knees.

"Stop!" I shout. He stills.

"I want to be on top."

He rubs his nose on mine then rolls off.

"Condom?"

"Side table."

I reach over, open the drawer and find a full box of condoms. "Wishful thinking?" I say with a smirk.

"A man can dream," he says with a big grin.

I quickly open it up and roll it down his impressive length. I climb over him and he offers me his hands. I take them and in one move I impale myself on him, letting out a scream of pure pleasure. I start to move immediately, and we find a rhythm that sends us both spiraling. His left hand is harshly gripping my hip and his right hand has traveled to my sex and has expertly found that bundle of nerves. It has been so long since a man has touched me that I come almost immediately. I don't think I have ever enjoyed sex enough with a man that he's brought me to orgasm. Usually, sex is so quick, there is not enough time for me to really enjoy it.

As I explode around him, I feel him shudder again and tense. Then I hear him yell, "Fuck, Brogan!" It startles me, and I sat stock-still, straddling him with his cock still inside me. He lifts his hand to caress my face and I roughly roll off him.

"Jesus Christ, Brogan! Give a guy a warning!" he yells as I pull off of him. He rolls to his side to look at me with concern on his face. "What's wrong, Brogan?" I just lay there unable to even look at his face. "Brogan, I just wanted to touch your face."

"I'm sorry," I say as I get up to grab my clothes.

"Brogan, stop. Come back here." He pats the bed.

"Kyren, it is late, and I need to get home." I can't look at him.

"For what, Brogan? There is no one there. Come back and curl up with me."

I finally look up at him, "That's just it, Kyren! I don't curl up, cuddle, spoon, or whatever afterglow word you might want to use!"

He's eyes soften to a lighter shade of blue. "Brogan, for tonight, we will do whatever you can handle. I don't want you to leave."

For tonight? Does that mean he wants more? He is so beautiful, as he looks at me. I don't really want to leave either. I drop my clothes and climb back into bed, lying on my side, facing him but not touching him.

"Kyren, I am so broken in so many ways, I…I don't think we should get any more involved," I whisper the last part.

"Well, less than five minutes ago, we were as involved as it gets," he says with a slight grin on his handsome face, like he's not quite sure how I will react.

I playfully slap his shoulder and laugh, hoping it will change the thick atmosphere in the room. He grabs his shoulder and acts wounded. Through laughter, I hear him mutter, "At least it wasn't the boys this time."

"I meant a relationship. Let's just take things slow and easy. That is all I can handle."

He lies back on his side, facing me. "I have admitted that I am unmistakably drawn to you in every way possible," he says, skimming down my body with his baby blues. "I don't want to push you. Just start by staying the night with me. Please."

He looks so damn inviting with his perfect smile. For the first time in my life, I really want to curl into his arms. I fight the unfamiliar urge.

"Can we just go to sleep?" I roll onto my back, hoping to avoid any more conversation for tonight.

"You don't want to talk about being so broken?"

"No."

He is leaning over me. I slowly, unsure of myself, reach up and touch his lips softly. He kisses my fingertips. Our eyes are locked and heated again.

"What do you want, baby?" he whispers.

"Just to lie beside you and feel safe."

"Can you turn around and curl into me? I won't touch you. I just want to feel you next to me."

The warmth in his eyes unravels me. I do as he asks, and he keeps his word. He doesn't snuggle into me. I relax and drift off to sleep.

Chapter 7

I can hear Zade screaming in the woods behind the house. I run to Daddy's closet and find the box where I have seen him hide his revolver. I check to make sure it's loaded. I take off running toward Zade's screams of agony. I'm yelling his name as I'm running. I hear him, telling me to go back. "Please, don't try and save me"!

I stop in my tracks for a second. I hear him scream out in pain again. I can't do as he asks. His screams are terrifying. I take off running again. I finally see him. There is blood everywhere. I start yelling, "Stop! Oh god, please stop! You're going to kill him!"

"Wake up! Wake up, Brogan!"

I am sitting straight up in bed. Tears are freely running down my face. I am wringing wet with sweat and Kyren is yelling at me to wake up, but he is not touching me.

"You're having a nightmare, baby. You're okay. You're safe in my bed." He suddenly grabs me and hugs me tight. This I can handle. No softness. I swipe at my tears. Then he starts to kiss me hard. I let him in. His mouth taste like my tears. He pushes me back on the bed. He breaks our heated kiss to gaze at me.

I whisper, "Don't think, Kyren. Just fuck me hard."

He inhales. "Oh, baby, your wish is my command." He leans up, and in one move, he is hard inside me. He roughly pulls out and slams into me again. One hand is steadying himself on the bed. He is pinching my nipple hard. God, it feels so good. I whimper.

He stills for a moment. "Brogan, look at me!" he barks. I obey his command. "Am I hurting you?" His voice is full of concern.

"God, no. Don't stop," I order back.

Then he really starts to move. I feel myself building. "Come, baby," he commands, and then he shifts his hips and pinches my nipple at the same time. I scream out as my orgasm explodes around him, and I feel him follow, whispering my name. After coming back to earth after my orgasm, he rolls to his side and draws me in tightly.

"Are you okay?"

"Yes, I am now," I say quietly.

"What was your dream about?"

"Old ghosts." I am so embarrassed. I need to remember to carry my Ambien with me for sleepovers.

His grip on me tightens, and he is inches from my ear. "Did I ever tell you I'm a ghost slayer, and I will rid you of all ghosts if you will let me?"

I melt into his arms. He is so sweet and yet so strong. "One day, maybe. For tonight, what we just did should scare all sorts of ghosts away." I giggle and wiggle my ass into him.

I feel him smile. "Keep that up, baby, and we will never sleep." He pulls me in tighter and kisses the back of my head. "Sleep, baby."

Chapter 8

I wake up to sunlight bursting through a crack in the curtains. I am alone, but I smell coffee. I am a total coffee junky. If I could hook coffee to an IV in my vein, I would be a happy woman. The door opens, and I grab the sheets to cover up.

"A little too late to be shy," Kyren says, smiling.

"Are you always this cheerful in the morning? If so, we are finished before we even get started," I say with a shy smile on my face and reach for the coffee he is sipping from. As I do, the sheet falls to my waist.

He stares at me. "You are beautiful," he says.

"Just give me the damn coffee," I growl.

"Nope." He has a big shit-eating grin on his face. "Kiss first." He puts the coffee mug on the bedside table, leans over, and barely brushes a kiss on my lips. Everything below my waist tightens. He sits on the side of the bed, grabs the coffee, and hands it to me. As he lets go of the mug, his hand brushes over my tattoo. "What does it say?"

It's a feather and along the inside stem is a saying, "Someday I will fly away."

He traces a finger over it. "Is this your motto?"

"No. It was my escape," I say softly, but watching his eyes for a reaction.

"When did you get it?"

“When I turned eighteen.”

“Who is Zade?” His eyes look vulnerable.

His question throws me off. “What?”

“Zade. You were yelling his name in your dream. Is he someone I need to be jealous of or someone’s ass I need to kick?” He is serious and glaring at me now. What happened to soft and sweet?

“Hold on, cowboy. Zade is my brother, so there will be no ass kicking.” The thought that he would be jealous really turns me on.

He pats me on the leg. “Good. I would hate to have to kick someone’s ass this early in the morning,” he says, grinning. He gets up, and I get a glorious look at his ass in his tight jeans, and it now dawns on me that he is fully dressed and smells clean.

I sit straight up. “Are you going somewhere?”

“I hate to leave you, but I have an early appointment. Help yourself to a shower and food.”

I am disappointed that he won’t be showering with me. I will consume a few more cups of coffee then shower. Cady is due home today anyway.

“Can I see you later?” he asks with a hopeful look in his eyes.

“Call me. I’m sure you already have the number,” I say with a smile.

I get up buck naked intending to find the coffee pot. He smacks me on the ass as I walk by him. I jump and laugh.

“That’s one fine ass you have there, Ms. Milby. And very tempting.”

I strut over to him, stand on my tiptoes and kiss his cheek and purposely rub against him. He growls and smacks me again. “You are such a bad girl. I may have to spank you for real later.”

I suck in air, Now I’m really hot, but I prefer that I spank him, but I don’t dare share my thoughts. He kisses me hard and pulls away. “Later, baby,” he says, and he is out the door.

Chapter 9

I run through my front door, trying to catch the ringing phone. I stumble and stub my toe on the door jam. "Fuck! That hurts!" I yell as I pick up the phone.

"Brogan, hello! Brogan, are you okay?"

I immediately straighten up. "Cady? Why are you calling? You should be walking in the door. Did something happen?"

"Did you trip in the doorway again?" I hear her laughing

"Not funny, Cady! What's wrong?"

"Nothing, honey. I'm just not ready to come home yet. I want to stay with Jon a few more weeks. I have already arranged a short leave of absence with work. But if you need me, honey, I will come home."

"Oh, Cady, don't be silly. I'm a grown woman, for Pete's sake. Well, most of the time. I'll be fine. I just miss you, and I have a lot to tell you."

"I miss you too, but what kind trouble did you get into in a week? You didn't actually bite the pizza man's ass, did you?"

I laugh at her overreaction. "I wanted to, but he ran too fast." She knows I'm teasing her and is laughing now too. I just blurt it out, "I met someone."

"What? Who?"

I proceed to tell her, not leaving out any details about Kyren.

"Wow! You didn't scare him off, and you didn't run for the hills. Sounds serious to me."

"Cady, you know me. I don't do serious, but I really like him. He is different from anyone I have ever met. He's going to call me later." There is pure excitement in my voice.

"Oh, honey. Go slow and easy."

Jeeze, she sounds just like Dr. Kohl. "Cady, I think we already went beyond slow and easy." We talk for a few more minutes, laughing like school girls. "I love you, Cady. Enjoy your time with Jon."

"I love you too, and Brogan…try to behave."

"What would be the fun in that?" I'm laughing, picturing her turning red.

"You are bad. Love you, honey. Bye." And we hang up.

On Saturday, I work out with my trainer and go to the shooting range on the mainland. I have been shooting for years, and I'm a good marksmen. As I am docking the boat, my cell phone rings. An unknown number. My heart skips a beat, and I decide to answer it. "Hello," I say a little sheepishly.

"Hey, baby."

"Kyren? You really are a stalker. I thought you would call the landline."

"I did, but you didn't answer."

"I don't even want to know how you got this number." Seriously, how did he get this number?

"So can I come over? I would love to meet your roommate."

A pang of jealousy hits me. I quickly dismiss it. "She decided to stay with Jon for a few more weeks, so your meeting her will have to wait."

"That means we will have the place to ourselves?" His tone turned to something feral.

"Yeeess." I'm all hot and bothered.

"We could make use of your outdoor kitchen and fireplace." He sounds so sexy with the low tone of his voice.

Two can play this game. "And maybe a few other places," I add in an equally sexy tone.

"Eager, aren't you?" he asks now laughing at me. Not the reaction I was looking for. "I'll be there by seven. I will bring wine."

"I prefer beer, Bud Light Lime."

"Do you now? Ms. Milby, I didn't peg you for a beer kinda girl."

"What kind of girl did you peg me for?" I ask, curious now.

"A kinky one." His voice is seductive again.

"Well, you are in luck, Mr. Nolan. I can definitely do kinky."

"I'll be there by six," he says quickly and hangs up. I laugh at the silence on the other end.

I finish up at the shooting range and run to the local market. I decide on a simple but delicious meal of baked cream cheese spaghetti with a Caesar salad with homemade dressing and rosemary olive loaf. I love to cook but don't get to very often. It crosses my mind that Kyren has his own cook, so I'm sure it won't be as good as of a meal as he is used to eating.

I make it home to put away the groceries, and there is time to spare for a shower. I am stumped on what to wear. I choose a short shimmery skirt with thigh-high stockings, no panties, and a sheer white long-sleeved blouse with a lacey dark gray bra. I turn around in the mirror to check out my outfit. That should work for him.

Even though I know I am clumsy in heels, I put on my three-inch black pumps. I sit down to put them on and then remember I stubbed my toe earlier. I squeeze my foot in and wince.

I brush out my long auburn hair and tuck it behind my ears. I put on faint shades of gray for eye shadow. The gray makes my lavender eyes pop. I feel sexy.

Dinner is just finishing up when the doorbell rings. Butterflies are instantly in my stomach. I gaze up at the clock, and it is exactly six o'clock. How does he do that? Did he sit outside the door until the exact time?

Before I open the door, I turn on some music by Pink. "Glitter in the Air" is playing. Limping to the door, I open it, and my mouth instantly waters and everything south is damp.

Kyren is holding flowers, dressed in tight black jeans, boots, and a tight black T-shirt that clings to every muscle. Temptation is his name.

"Wow, you look edible." I'm sure my mouth is still hanging open. Get it together, girl. Play it cool. Don't seem too damn eager. Eager? Hell, I could eat him up.

He smiles a shy smile and hands me the flowers. "You look pretty amazing yourself." He twirls his finger in the air, indicating for me to turn around. I gladly and seductively comply.

"Sheer is definitely my friend," he says, drooling.

"Won't you come in, Mr. Nolan?" I bat my eyes at him. "Thank you for the flowers. I don't think anyone has ever given me flowers." I don't have the heart to tell him that I'm not the flowers kind of girl. I would like to remind him that I am the kinky kind of girl, but I guess I should let the poor man in the house before I jump his bones. Surely, Cady has a vase. Jon is always sending her flowers. I turn and limp over to the kitchen in search of a vase.

"Brogan…why are you limping?" he asks with concern in his voice. Even that sounds hot. Focus, focus.

"Ms. Graceful that I am, stubbed my toe trying to get in the door earlier to answer the phone."

"So…why are you wearing those shoes?" He is pointing and grinning at me.

"I wanted to impress you." I shrug and smile.

"The only place those would impress me is around my ears, so take them off," he commands.

Oh my, he has me so turned on, and he has only just walked in the door. I swallow and regain my composure. I smile up at him and slip them slowly off my feet. "I would like them around your ears with my feet in them." We share a heated stare before I break our silence. "I hope you don't mind. I cooked instead of eating out."

"Why would I mind?" He looks confused.

"Well, um…I'm sure you are used to gourmet meals with your own personal cook."

He gives me smile. "I'll go get the beer." Before he opens the door, he turns. "This song is so you," he says with a smirk.

I will have to pay more attention to the words and see if I see the same connection. He returns with a small cooler. "I'll just put this on the porch."

"Are you drinking beer with me?"

"Yes, but not that shit. I don't really care for beer, so I settled on a Michelob. I am a wine guy and a kinky guy all rolled into one." He is teasing me, but for some reason, he makes me blush. That has never happened.

"Go ahead and pop the bottles, and I will bring out the food."

"I will light the fireplace." He turns, and I get a glimpse of his ass. I could so bite that.

It is a beautiful night for a fire. I walk out with the plates of food, and he pulls my chair out for me. Polite and kinky. What more could a girl want.

"The food looks great," he says, already digging in.

I'm starving. Just realizing that I had been too busy to eat all day. I join him and I'm not very ladylike as I scarf down a mouthful of food. "How was your day, honey?" I ask with a laugh.

He stops mid-chew. "Do you really want to know or are you just making conversation? Food is great, by the way. I must give Mrs. Moore your recipe."

I think about his question for a minute. Even though I'm making light conversation, I really want to know about his day. I tilt my head and look at him. "Yes, I really want to know." Does he think I only want one thing? Maybe I should play a little harder to get.

His eyes gleam, and in between bites, he tells me about the layout of the yacht he has been working on. I can tell he really enjoys his work; there is so much excitement in his voice. I am so engrossed in what he is saying that I almost didn't hear him ask me about my day. I tell him. This just seems so normal to me, well, what my idea of what normal would be.

We finish our meals and move to sit in front of the fireplace. I already have pillows and blankets on the ground.

"Dinner was great. Thank you."

Why does he make me blush? I just smile at him. He is just so full of compliments. Compliments have never set well with me. He hands me another beer, and we sit down both curled up in our own blankets.

He leans over. "Have you ever made out by this fireplace?" His eyes are a shade darker.

"No," I say, leaning toward him. "Cady has a fiancé, and she won't let me kiss her," I say, laughing. I haven't had any men in my home, well, minus the pizza man. And I think he is afraid of me."

"Afraid of you?" he asks with eyebrows raised.

"Yea. Cady told him I made a comment about wanting to bite his ass so that he could protect it from me."

"Lucky man," he says, laughing. "At least you didn't want to knee him in the balls."

"How many times do I need to apologize?" I ask, gaping at him.

"Oh, baby, that is something a man never forgets." He is still laughing at me. "There will be no more longing for the pizza man's ass, but you can bite mine anytime."

Bastard. "I'm sure, given enough time in this relationship, that will happen." It is my turn to tease him.

"Relationship, huh?" he says in all seriousness.

"Um, um, I um…" I fail to articulate any real words. Why did I say relationship? I am so fucking stupid. Great way to scare a man off, especially one I really like.

"It's okay," he says with a wicked gleam in his eyes. "I'm just teasing you. I want a relationship with you, if you will let me." He looks vulnerable.

I really do like this man. He's hot, funny, smart, and did I mention hot? And, oh yes, he seems to handle all my shit really well. "I would like to try." He is staring at me hard when I realize I said that out loud. Shit, say something. "I'm not sure how good I will be at it, but you make me want to try." I say in a soft voice, very unsure of myself or where that came from. "But I have issues. Some of which you have already witnessed."

"We all have issues, baby. They make us who we are."

"But, but…why do you want to be with me?" I look down at the hands I am wringing together.

He pulls at my chin to meet his eyes. “You are a beautiful, strong, intelligent, sarcastic, kinky woman. What’s not to love?” His eyes have deepened in color again.

“Love? You can’t love me, Kyren. You don’t even really know the real me.”

He holds my chin firmly in place, not letting me look away. “Baby, I fell in love with you at the festival.” His face is so serious.

“Really?” I say wide-eyed. I think with fear.

“I have told you I am drawn to you and I can’t walk away.”

I swallow hard at his words. “Tell me something? How old are you? Twenty-eight, thirty years old?”

“I’m thirty-two. Why?” he says, squinting his eyes at me.

“Well, you are gorgeous, obviously successful, smart, funny. Any woman would latch onto you. Why are you unattached?”

“Any woman including you?” His eyes darken. “I haven’t always been unattached.”

There is that jealousy sparing its evil head again. “Oh, do tell.”

“I had a girlfriend in college, and when I dropped out, I went into the army for two years. When I came back, I bought the marina and started building yachts. Somewhere in that time frame, we grew apart. She said I never had time for her.” He pauses. “She was right. My love was for my work not her. So we said our good-byes.”

“So you have time now with a fucked-up, kinky woman?”

“Yes,” he says without hesitation.

Holy fuck! He really wants to be with me. I swallow hard again. “You need to know some things about me before you can make a decision like that.”

“Lay it on me, sugar,” he says, parroting a line in Pink’s song.

I turn so I can fully face him. “Well, you already know I like control during sex, and you know about the nightmares.”

“Yes,” he says, staring into my eyes. “That will change over time with me.”

“Don’t bet on it. I’ve been this way for years.”

“Have a little faith, sugar.”

“What you need to know is why I am this way, and then you will leave me. So why don’t we quit before we are in too deep.” I look away.

He grabs my chin again. “Don’t bet on it,” he says, mimicking my words back to me.

“I have been going to counselors since I was eighteen. The one I am with now, I have been with for four years. My longest male relationship besides Zade,” I say teasingly, trying to lighten the mood a little. “As far as shrinks go, I really like him. But don’t tell him I said that. He has done wonders for my brother. He has not only helped him survive, he’s given him his life back. For that, I am eternally grateful.”

“Have you let him help you?”

“As much as I let anyone,” I mutter. I take in a long-needed breath. “My dad started drinking when I was eight years old. At least, that is the earliest I remember. He began to beat my mom quiet frequently. Zade is four years older than me and remembers a lot more. Zade would try to stop him, and he would get beat too. I was so scared, I would hide in my closet to keep from hearing their screams. One day, I got brave enough to come out and try to help, but Zade physically shoved me back into the closet."

Another deep inhale. "When I was twelve, Zade took me out and taught me how to shoot a gun and a shotgun. We would sneak into Dad's closet and get his guns and practice while he wasn't around. Zade would get some older kids to buy the ammo, and we always made sure to clean them and put them back exactly where we found them."

"Mom by now was drunk or high all the time. It was the only way she could cope. She couldn't protect herself, much less us. When I was fourteen, Dad had come home one night, drunk as usual, and started in on my mom. I could hear her crying for him to stop. I crawled out of bed to check on her. He was punching her in the face, but I heard her whisper to go back into my room. Dad stopped and reached for me. He had this sick smile on his face. He said he would leave Mom alone if I would go with him out into the barn and help him with something. I remember his voice being very calm." I hesitate and look up at Kyren.

"Keep going," he says quietly.

"When I went with him into the barn, he started telling me how much he loved me, and that I was so precious and so beautiful. He said that I was his angel. I remember the feel of him softly caressing my arms, slowly, up and down. The look on his face was terrifying; it didn't match the gentle touch.

"Suddenly, he grabbed me and pushed me against a wall that was lined with different types of farm tools and ropes. I screamed for him to stop and fought him, but he was too strong. He tied my wrists together and hooked me to the wall. I was kicking and screaming the entire time. My wrists were bleeding.

"After watching me struggle and finally give out, he was gentle again with his words and his touch. I was hoping at that point he would just beat me or kill me. The gentleness, I could not take. I wished for Zade to save me.

"He was in the middle of raping me when my mother stumbled into the barn. She tried to get him off me, but he backhanded her. She fell backward and hit her head hard. I remember hearing the crack of her skull. At that point, I became numb. Blood was streaming down my arms, but I no longer felt the pain of what he had done to me. He reached up, untied me, cradled me, then stepped over Mom and took me into the house.

"He laid me gently on the couch, and as soon as he walked away, I ran back into the barn. She was barely conscious. She just kept saying she was so sorry. I helped her up and took her into Zade's room, but he wasn't there. I tucked her into Zade's bed. I hurried past my parent's room to the bathroom. I could already hear my father snoring. I quickly shut the bathroom door and locked it behind me. I jumped in the shower and started crying. I wanted that bastard off my skin. I scrubbed so hard, I was bleeding again.

"I snuck out of the shower and ran past his room again and stood just outside the door. He was passed out cold. I figured we were safe for now. I just wish I knew where Zade was. I went into my room and locked the door. I slept in the closet that night.

"The next thing I remember, I was woken up by Zade yelling something. After that, things got a little hazy. I remember crawling out of the closet. It was morning. I snuck out of my room and walked into the bathroom. Mom was lying on the floor. I thought she was passed out again. There were several empty bottles of liquor lying next to her. She had had enough and killed herself."

I feel Kyren squeeze my hand, and it is the first time I have looked up at him since I began my story. Tears are streaming down his face. He composes himself with a big inhale. "Is that all of it?" he asks in a trembling voice.

"No." I swallow and continue my nightmare.

"Dad was never blamed for her death by the police. He had threatened me that if I uttered one word about what he had done, he would hurt Zade. So I said nothing. I never even told Zade."

"Zade was eighteen and planning our escape. I later found out that Dad had told Zade that if he left, he would hunt us down and take it out on me. Zade believed him. Zade had taken a part-time job and was trying to hold back enough money for a bus ticket out of town. Most of his money was spent on buying us food. We were lucky to eat once a day."

"I came home from school one day and found mine and Zade's clothes in bags. The house was a mess, and chairs were knocked over. Shattered glass was all over the floor. I found out later that Zade had finally saved enough money for our escape, and we were leaving when I came home from school. Dad had come home unexpectedly and figured out what Zade was up to. He went mad and fought with Zade. Zade had put up a struggle, but Dad was just so much bigger and stronger. He knocked Zade unconscious.

"I heard blood curdling screams coming from the woods behind our house. I ran into Dad's closet and grabbed his revolver. I made sure it was loaded, and I took off running as fast as I could to the harrowing screams. Dad had Zade tied to a tree and was beating him with a whip. He was a bloody mess. I slid the revolver firmly in my hands. I yelled for him to stop. Zade screamed for me to run. He couldn't see the gun. Dad stopped and turned toward me. He started laughing. He sounded possessed.

"'My precious little girl would never shoot her daddy.' He took a step toward me.

"I knew I had five shots and I had to make them count. I aimed and pulled the trigger, shooting him in the right thigh. He crumbled in agony. He was screaming, 'I can't believe you shot me.'

"I quickly ran over to Zade and frantically untied him. I put my arms around him and held him up to walk. Somehow Dad had managed to get on his feet and was moving toward us, cracking his whip. I knew in that instant I had to kill him. It was our only chance of survival. Zade saw my intent in my eyes. He grasped the gun with me, and together, we pulled the trigger.

"Dad went stumbling back. We had shot him in the chest. He had blood pouring out, and he wasn't moving. He was dead. The monster was finally dead. I was filled with relief and numb at the same time. Zade went into big brother mode. We left his body in the woods and went back to the house. We cleaned and bandaged Zade's wounds, collected our clothes. Zade set the house on fire, and we fled. We never looked back. I flew away that day."

I let out a deep exhale and felt tears roll down my face. I had not cried about it since the day it happened. "Kyren, say something. I just told you I murdered my father."

Silence.

"I understand if it's too much to handle and you never want to see me again, but please say something." It was a plea.

"Brogan." His voice was cracking, "Baby, he got what he deserved. I would have done the same thing after I had beaten the shit out of him. Killing him was kindness in comparison to him being ripped apart."

I gulped back tears. "So you're not going to leave?"

"No baby, I'm not going anywhere." He leans over and grabs me to hold me, and I let him.

"You're safe. I will never let anyone harm you again. That *is* a promise." He says each word slowly so that he knows I understand him and believe him. He continues to hold me for a few moments before he speaks again. "That explains a lot why you want control and why you hate tenderness and compliments. For now, I will try and give you what you need, but at some point, you will have to trust me. I'm the kind of man who likes to dominate during sex."

"Thank you," I whisper. "I will try too."

I don't know how long we sat there holding each other in silence. I drifted off to sleep in his arms. When I woke in the morning, I find myself wrapped in blankets and still outside. The fireplace is still burning. Kyren has either gotten up early to restart it, or he never slept. I sit and see Kyren standing at the end of the dock. I stand up, straighten my skirt, wrap myself back in my blanket, and head for Kyren. Fear consumes me. What if he has had second thoughts?

"You are still here." It's a statement, not a question.

"Yes, baby, I'm still here."

"Did you sleep?"

"No, I watched you sleep. I wanted to be awake if you had any nightmares. Bringing up old ghosts tend to do that."

I frown. He's right. For the first time in a long time, my ghosts didn't haunt me. Kyren walks close to me and brushes his nose with mine. Nothing else touches me.

"I made coffee for the caffeine beast in you."

I smile. I look up at him and lock with those beautiful pale blue eyes. "I'd rather shower with you."

He closes his eyes, and when he opens them, they are the color of a storm. He doesn't say anything. He just takes my hand and leads the way

"May I undress you?" he asks with his hands lifted in the air waiting for my response.

"Yes," I say hoarsely.

He starts unbuttoning my blouse. He untucks it from my skirt and slowly slides it off my shoulders. I have goosebumps over his tenderness. I fight the urge to grab his hands. As if he knows what I'm thinking, he leans close to my ear and whispers, "You're safe with me, baby." He bites my earlobe, and I feel it way down deep inside. I gasp. He then unzips my skirt, sliding it down my legs. I am left standing in my bra and thigh highs.

I hear his inhale. "No panties, Ms. Milby. I love it and these." He rubs his hands around the lace, holding up my stockings. "Sexy as hell," he growls.

I clinch my legs together. "Enough," I say a little too loudly. He steps back, lifting his hands in surrender.

"My turn to undress you."

"I'm all yours, baby."

I grip the hem of his shirt and rip it off over his head. His turn to suck in air. Luckily, he has already removed his socks and boots. I walk round him and close my eyes. I reach around him so that my front is pressed flat against his back. I rub the muscles of his chest and abdomen. I slowly unbutton his jeans and slid my hand inside to find him insanely hard. This time, he growls deep in his throat as I grasp his shaft, stroking him roughly up and down.

"Baby, I'm not going to last long with you touching me like that."

I smile against his shoulder blade. I release him and reach around unhook my bra, letting it fall to the floor. I put my arms back around him and rub my breasts with its hardened nipples against his back. He growls again and quickly turns around in my arms. He kisses me hard, and I feel his hands running down my legs, slowly removing my stockings as he goes. He stands back, and I grab his jeans and boxers and hurriedly pull them off. "Stay right here," I rasp out. "I'll be right back."

I run to my room and open my side table drawer and grab what I came for and go back to Kyren. The shower is running. He turns to see what I have come back with.

"So, what kind of toy have you brought for me, baby?"

"It's a cat-o'-nine." It's a small leather whip with multiple tails.

"I am well aware of what it is and how to use it," he says with his hand extended.

"Um, it's for me to use on you," I say a little shyly.

"I could bring you great pleasure with that," he says, smiling.

I don't want to know how he knows how to use it. I choose to let the thought pass. "I want to bring you pleasure."

"All you had to do was show up, and I have extreme pleasure." I smile a wicked smile at him and then I swat him in the ass with the cat-o-nine. "Bring it on," he taunts me.

"Turn around," I command him. And when he does, I see his scars that mar his back. I had forgotten about them. I immediately drop the cat-o-nine to the floor.

"What is wrong, baby?" His eyes are scanning me.

"Um…I had forgotten someone has caused you pain with a whip. I'm so sorry." My lip starts to quiver.

"No no. Baby, baby, don't cry. It's not the same. I will tell you about it, but not now." He grabs my hair and starts kissing me hard. He lifts me up and steps into the shower with me. My legs are wrapped around his waist, and I am pressed against the tile wall. His head trails down my breasts, sucking and biting my nipples hard. I groan out in pleasure and in pain. This is what I need. I need to feel the pain. It's what I want, and I enjoy the pain and pleasure. Before I realize it, he is kneeling in front of me, spreading my legs apart.

"Oh, baby, you taste so sweet," he says as he dips his tongue inside me. I jump at the sensation. No man has ever touched me with his mouth down there. It's a sweet sensation. I grab his hair with both my hands and pull hard.

He growls up at me. "Please let me," he says with his lips glistening from me. I loosen my grip, and this time he sucks and licks harder. It doesn't take long for me to explode into a glorified orgasm. I yell his name.

He stands in front of me, his eyes locked with mine. He holds his cock in his left hand stroking it. "Do you want this, baby?"

"Yes," I gasp.

"Turn around."

I hesitate, but I give him this.

"Bend over. Hands against the wall." Just his command has me panting for more. I have never allowed anyone to command me during sex. This is totally hot with him.

I feel him spread my legs and then he smacks me hard on the ass. I yelp.

"Hush, baby," he rasps. I can tell his fighting for control. He suddenly thrusts into me, slamming me into the wall. He stills. "Too much?" he asks between clenched teeth.

"Fuck, no," I say between gasps of air.

"Today, I will fuck you hard, baby, but one day soon, I will make slow and gentle love to you," he says then he slams into me again.

This is so erotic. As he continues his pace, he reaches around with his hand and rubs my clit. His other hand is intermittently stroking and slapping my ass.

"Come for me, baby!" he roars out, barely containing himself. I explode pulsating around his cock that is buried deep inside me. He comes hard calling out my name. We sink to the bottom of the shower together exhausted. Sprays of water roll over us, bringing us back to earth. I am sitting on his lap, and he is still inside me. I vaguely feel him biting my shoulder.

"Are you okay, baby?"

"Mmmmm," is all I can manage to get out.

He laughs.

I manage to turn myself around, keeping him tucked inside me. He winces, but I feel him getting hard again. I slowly start to ride him and then increase my pace. I pull his hair again. It only takes a minute, and he comes again. This time, yelling, "Oh fuck, Brogan!"

"Are you okay, baby?" I ask, mimicking his earlier question.

"Mmmmm," is his response, and I start to laugh a deep, cathartic laugh. The best thing is that he starts laughing with me.

We are now curled up together in the bottom of the shower floor. Me lying on top of him. I'm getting cold, and goosebumps are forming.

"Let's get out, baby, before you catch a cold."

I reach up and turn off the water and begin my very unladylike climb off the shower floor.

"Don't fall, baby," he reaches out and steadies me.

We wrap each other in big, fluffy towels. He dries my hair as I dry his beautiful body.

We decide to take my boat out and go fishing for what's left of our day. I pack up some food, and Kyren refills our cooler with ice and restocks the beer.

We load up and take the boat out into the gulf, just past the pier where I know there will be good fishing. On the ride out, we are both very quiet, each in our own heads. I have shared with him everything, and he is still here. I am in awe of him, and at the same time, I am frightened of my feelings for him. Not only on how quickly I have fallen for him, but of how much I feel for him. I can't let myself get hurt by him. I need to quit thinking about it so much and enjoy the beautiful man in front of me.

I am dying to touch him. I purposely bump into him several times, and I grin at him from ear to ear. The silence is finally broken. "I know what you are doing," he says, smiling.

"What?" I ask innocently, batting my eyes.

“Flirting with me.” He is still smiling.

“Me? No.”

He casts his line, and I reach down and pull my cover-up over my head, revealing a very skimpy bikini. He nearly falls off the boat. I love that I have such an effect on him. “Kyren, be careful,” I say, laughing.

“Don’t do that when a man is casting,” he says, staring at me like a man that wants to eat me.

“Breathe, baby. It’s not like you haven’t seen me or done wicked things with me before.” Suddenly, I realize I called him baby. I turn crimson and decide my only escape is the water, so I jump in. The water is cold, and as I come up, I am greeted with a splash. Kyren had pulled off all his clothes and jumped in with me. How does the man undress so quickly?

“Are you crazy?” I screech out, giggling.

“Only for you, baby, and you cannot escape me.” He pulls me in for a long hard kiss.

When we finally break apart, we swim around and dive underwater like two young children. It’s refreshing. I haven’t acted like a child since I was eight. It feels good.

I attempt to climb back into the boat, but Kyren pulls me back in on top of him, and then climbs over me to get to the ladder.

I yell, “Oh no, you don’t, mister,” and I grab him, pulling myself onto his back, trying to climb into the boat first. He lets go of the ladder, and we both go back into the cold ocean. We both come up, sputtering and laughing.

He swims up next to me. "Okay, ladies first," he concedes. I splash him playfully and climb into the boat, wiggling my ass as I climb. As he starts climbing the ladder, I remember he is naked and there are other boats not far from us.

"Umm, Kyren? Clothes?"

Without any modesty at all, he continues his climb into the boat.

I am roaring in laughter at him. "I am not driving you back until you are clothed, mister. You have already blinded the nearby boaters with your nudity. I will not traumatize my neighbors too."

He places his hands on his chest, acting offended. "I am crushed. Besides, I'll take my chance because you have no neighbors."

The bastard. He is grinning. I take his jeans and throw them at him. "Just put your pants on!" I can't help but laugh at him.

"If you insist, Ms. Milby, but remember, when you want them off later, you ordered me to put them on. Besides, I will give in because I am starving."

We enjoy our picnic on the boat, and I have way too many beers, so Kyren drives us back in.

"You have had too much to drink." He is grinning.

"Kyren, please stay the night with me."

"Are you begging Ms. Drunk Milby?"

I straighten up, a little offended. "No, I don't beg." Then I glance up at his smiling face and realized he is teasing me.

"It's okay, baby. I wasn't planning on leaving you tonight, but I do have to leave early in the morning for an appointment, so don't be surprised if I am long gone before you open those beautiful lavender eyes of yours."

I can build us a soft pallet on the floor, pop popcorn, and put in movie."

"Popcorn with butter and parmesan?" He sounds hopeful. I grin up at him. "Is there any other way?"

He frowns. "No chick flicks."

"Let's watch something blow up." Now I'm hopeful.

"Deal," he says and swats my ass.

"Hey! Deals are sealed with handshakes not swats on the ass." I rub my ass.

He grabs me and places both his hands on my ass. "Why would I want to shake your hand when I can cop a feel of your fine ass?" He kisses me then releases me. "I was promised popcorn. Go, wench, and pop."

We curl up on the floor like children, creating tents in the living room. Kyren has chosen the latest *Die Hard* movie.

Neither one of us are watching the movie. We are lying, facing one another, taking turns feeding each other popcorn. This is the most intimate I have ever been with anyone. I watch him as he talks. He face and expressions are beautiful. His face and eyes just light up. Is he always this way or is it just me? I don't really know much about this beautiful man. I want to know more, but a day in the sun has caught up with me, and I nod off into a deep and restful sleep.

Chapter 10

I wake to a bright light shining in and no Kyren lying beside me. I can't remember every having such a good night's sleep. I smell coffee, so I get my hopes up that maybe he is in the shower. I roll toward the kitchen and glance at the clock that says 10:05. I jump up. I have never slept so late. I call Kyren's name, but there is no answer and I don't hear the water running. I get up and head for the coffee pot. There is a note on the counter.

Good morning, baby. I told you I had to leave early. I made a fresh pot of coffee for my caffeine monster. I'm sorry I didn't wake you to tuck you in bed last night, but you looked so peaceful, I didn't want to move you. Thank you for this weekend. It was awesome. The sex was mind blowing. I miss you already.

Come by later.

XOXOX

Kyren.

I'm sure I have a stupid smile on my face as I finish reading his note. As I drink my coffee, it really hits me. What have I done? How did I let this man get to me so easily? I don't want a relationship. Sex. Hot sex, yes, but this feels scary. Have I lost my mind? I don't want him falling for me. I am too fucked up. I have nothing to give him back. Yes, this was an amazing weekend of flirting and sex, but that has to be it. I have to make that clear to him.

My thoughts are interrupted by my cell phone ringing. I scramble to answer it because very few people have my number. I briefly wonder again how Kyren got it. I glance at the number before answering it. It's Zade.

"Hey, big brother," I say cheerfully.

"Hey, Brogan, I'm coming for a visit to your little island.

I'm quiet.

"Brogan?"

"Zade, do you think that's a good idea?" I feel terrible for even asking him, but I remember what happened last time we visited.

"Yes, Brogan, I do. It's time. We both need this. Besides, I really miss you."

I do love my brother, but our entire lives together had been painful, and Zade has made so much progress. I don't want him to have another break down.

"Brogan, are you still there?"

"Yes," I whisper.

"Look, I know what you are thinking, but I am 100 percent better.

I am ashamed to admit it. "Maybe it is me that I am worried about," I say softly.

"I know, Brogan, but we are all each other has. We need to heal together."

"When are you coming?"

"Two weeks from today."

I'm silent.

"How is Cady?"

"She is good. She's staying with Jon for a while. I'm not sure she can make herself leave him. She is so over the top in love with him."

"I'm glad she is happy, but I know she has been your anchor. Are you okay with her gone?"

"Yes, Zade, I'm fine." What I really want to tell him is about Kyren, but I have just convinced myself that it is just sex, so there really is nothing to tell. "I really do want to see you, Zade."

"Good. I was hoping you would be open. Besides, I have already booked my flight. I will e-mail you the flight schedule.

"Okay. Zade?"

"What is it ,baby girl?"

I almost tear up at his endearment. "I love you."

"I know. I love you too, Brogan. I will see you soon."

Zade knows all too well how hard those three words are for me. Progress.

I hang up and call Cady. She sounds so happy. I tell her all about my weekend with Kyren and then about my decision to tell him it's just great sex.

"No, Brogan, you can't. Please, sweetie. Just give him a chance. He has already gotten to you more than any other man. He sounds perfect for you."

"But, Cady, I have only known him for a few days."

"Who cares? Do you like him?"

"We have great sex together, and so far, he is not weirded out by me wanting to be in control."

"Brogan, I didn't ask about the sex. I asked if you like him?"

"Yes," I say as I inhale.

"When is the last time you, Ms. Cranky, have liked anyone?"

"Never," I say flatly.

"My point exactly. Just take it a day at a time, sweetie."

"I may regret it."

"And you may not."

Zade is right. She is my anchor. "Cady, I have nothing to give him. I am not worthy of a man like him."

"Oh, Brogan. You are worth a million. You just don't see it. Give him and yourself a chance."

My voice of reason. "Okay," I say and exhale.

We talk for a few minutes longer about what she and Jon have been up to. Before we hang up, I tell her about Zade's plan to visit. She, of course, thinks it's a great idea.

"I will see you in a few weeks, Cady." We hang up. I do feel better about Kyren. Cady always has a way of making me see things different.

I quickly shower and dress in white shorts without the panties and a snug, strappy emerald-green top. I dry my hair and pause in front of the mirror. I never like looking directly at my reflection. I can always see what's on the inside. I feel so exposed. I stand still as

I truly try to see what Kyren sees in me. I am very tone from kickboxing. My breasts are a perky 36C. I'm tall with curves and long legs. I have never stopped to think if I was beautiful or not because I know what's on the inside. I think I might be pretty until lavender eyes lock with lavender eyes in the mirror. I see through them. They are my mothers. I see weakness and fragility. I see someone who gave up on life. A single tear flows down my cheek. I wish my mother could have been stronger and protect us and herself. But she was lost and weak.

I dry my face and apply eye shadow, mascara, and lip gloss. I'm not big on makeup, but today, I want to feel pretty. Pretty for Kyren. His name on my lips makes me smile.

I slip on my flip-flops and I am out the door, with only one destination in mind. I have mapped out in my mind how to get to the marina by boat. This is one skill that has come very natural to me. Zade and I use to map out escape routes. The day is beautiful, and the water is calm and for the first time in a long time. I feel hopeful.

As I get closer to the marina, I see Kyren with two other men. They appear to be looking at blueprints. Kyren is shirtless, and it is very distracting. My skin tingles in reaction. He catches a glimpse at me and waves and points to where he wants me to dock the boat. Kyren leaves the other two men to assist me.

"Hey, baby. I'm glad you came. I have someone I want you to meet." Kyren pulls me out of the boat and draws me in for a deep kiss.

"Hey, yourself," I say as he releases me breathless.

As we tie off the boat he tells me his Uncle Tom is out of his man cave today, and he wants to meet me.

"Oh, that's, ummm, kind of like meeting the parents," I say while fidgeting. I am suddenly very anxious, and Kyren picks up on it right away.

"Hey, it's okay, baby," he says as if he has read my mind. "He is going to love your smart, beautiful mouth." The bastard is grinning at me.

"Okay, that compliment was too painfully laced with sarcasm." Now he is just laughing at me. Double bastard!

"Well, I count two people over there. Who is the other one?"

"I'm glad to see that in your nervousness, you haven't lost your ability to count. He is the gentleman I am building the new yacht for that I told you about."

I pinch him in the chest. "And I'm the sarcastic one?" He rubs his chest and then he kisses me again.

We turn to head where they were standing, and one man is climbing in his truck and leaving. If I'm lucky, maybe it was his uncle. I notice Kyren does not attempt to hold my hand as we walk. I think he is trying to be sensitive to my feelings, but I am missing the warmth of his touch.

No such luck. "You must be Brogan. Kyren hasn't shut up about you all morning. Kinda hard for a man to get some work done when he doesn't quit yapping."

Oh, I already like this man. He gives Kyren shit, and Kyren looks embarrassed. "Thanks a lot, Uncle Tom, for making me sound like a teenage girl!"

"Well, if the shoe fits…" I am laughing at Kyren's expense as I reach to shake his uncle's hand.

"It's very nice to meet you, Mr.…?

"Uncle Tom will do." He has a shit- eating grin on his handsome face.

"Uncle Tom," I repeat. Something has suddenly made me very uneasy and queasy. A scent, a nauseating smell. Cologne. My face must be white as a ghost.

Kyren grabs my shoulders.

"Brogan, what is it? What's wrong?" He is frowning at me.

I swallow hard as to not vomit on his shoes. I try to breathe deep and push back the demons. "Nothing," I say, trying to regain my composure.

"Have you had anything to eat other than a pot of coffee?"

"No. That must be it. I'm just hungry." It's only a little lie. I haven't eaten, but I know that really isn't the problem.

Uncle Tom steps up and extends his elbow for me to take it. "Then let's go feed the girl. We can't have her falling off the dock before I have even had a chance to find out what she sees in you," he says as he nudges Kyren.

He leads the way up to Kyren's yacht but stops just outside the entrance. "This is as far as I go, missy."

"Oh, right! Kyren told me you don't like boats or water."

“Nope. Not a fan, so I will let you get your belly full, and we can chat later so that I can embarrass my nephew more.” He is winking at me.

“Thanks, Uncle Tom. We will be sure to find you later,” Kyren says, words dripping with sarcasm.

I have recovered fully and grin at his uncle. “I look forward to that conversation.” Kyren has already walked in and has asked Mrs. Moore to bring us some lunch and a bottle of champagne.

“Are we celebrating something?”

“I am celebrating the fact that you actually came over and did not run.”

“That is something to celebrate,” I say under my breath because the truth is I was very close until I talked to Cady.

“What was that about outside? You look like you saw a ghost.”

“Not saw, smelled.”

“What?”

“My father use to wear an identical cologne that I remember too well. I’m sure it was just my imagination.”

“It’s funny how a smell can take you back.”

“Maybe Uncle Tom wears the same cologne. I will speak to him about it.”

“Don’t be silly. You can’t ban his cologne because it brings back bad memories for me. It just caught me off guard. I haven’t smelled it in a long time. I’m okay, really.” It’s sweet that he wants to protect me.

"All right, let's open the champagne," he says, seemingly appeased.

"Do you have orange juice?"

"Mimosas?" He is snarling.

"Yes, obviously you don't like them," I say, laughing at him.

"No, but for you, I will drink one. I will return with OJ."

As he turns to walk away, he grabs his shirt. Dammit. I was enjoying the view. It dawns on me how comfortable he is with himself even with his scars showing. My scars aren't visible, but I'm so uncomfortable with myself. He is beautiful even despite them. I wonder when he is going to tell me how they got there, or who hurt him so badly. I have decided not to ask him about them again. I know better than anyone. If he's not ready, I don't want to push. Lost in my thoughts, I have walked over to a wall with pictures. It looks like a young Kyren with maybe his mom and dad.

I jump when I feel a hand touch my shoulder. "Damn, Kyren! You are very stealthy like for a big guy."

"I'm sorry," he says, leaning close to my ear. "I will start announcing when I walk into a room. I guess, me calling out your name wasn't enough," he says leaning back and frowning.

"I'm sorry. I guess I'm just a little jumpy."

He hands me my mimosa, and he is still frowning at me. "Not too much until you have food in your stomach. I don't want you drunk. Yet." His frown has turned into a mischievous smile.

I turn back to the pictures. "Are these your parents?" I turn back to look at him.

"Yes." I see a little sadness creep into his beautiful baby blues. "This was taken two years before they died."

"I'm so sorry, Kyren." I softly rub his arm.

"Don't be. I have only good memories of them."

I continue to stroke his arm. "I'm sure you must miss them."

"I miss Mom singing to me every night at bedtime. I miss my dad teaching me how to fish. He was a very patient man." I see a soft smile cross his face.

"I'm glad you have good memories of them, but didn't that make it harder to lose them?"

"No. It made me grateful for the time I had with them."

I haven't realized I have spoken my thoughts out loud. "I think it was easier on me because I hated mine."

"You hated your mom too?" Now he is rubbing my arm.

"What?"

"You said you hated them."

Now I'm embarrassed. "I'm sorry, Kyren. I didn't realize I said that out loud." I turn away from him, and he turns me back to face him.

"I understand you hating your dad, but why your mom?" He is staring at me, willing me to answer his question.

I pause for a moment trying to draw up what real emotion I felt for her. I haven't felt anything for her in so long. "I…I didn't hate her. I felt so many different emotions about her, but no, hate wasn't one of them."

"She didn't protect you." It's a statement, not a question.

"No, she couldn't. She was too weak." I hang my head at the admission.

Kyren lifts my chin up toward him. "I'm sure she loved you."

"Can we change the subject, please? I'm starving."

Kyren leans over and places a firm kiss on my forehead and whispers, "You are safe with me, baby."

"I don't need you to save me," I say a little too harshly. "I'm not some weak, fragile little girl."

"No, you certainly are not," he says as he leads me to the table.

There is a whole spread of food on the table from fresh fruit to sandwiches. "Mrs. Moore is amazing. Is she always this prepared for uninvited guests?"

"You are never uninvited, and yes, she keeps us stocked very well."

I sit and dive in. I am really hungry. I lift my glass to Kyren. "Cheers." We toast, and I gulp down my entire drink. Kyren just laughs at me. Between bites of food, I tell him about Zade coming for a visit.

"Are you okay with him visiting?"

"Of course, I am," I say a little hesitantly. "He's my brother. I just want us to be okay."

"You have doubts?"

"It's just, last time, he had a breakdown." Kyren remains silent. "But he's better now." I look down and rub my thighs.

"What?" he asks, looking concerned.

"It's just that I always thought Zade was the strong one, and when he broke down…well, it was just very difficult for me to see him like that. He wanted so much to protect me…when I killed our father, he blamed himself for my pulling the trigger."

"You both pulled the trigger."

"I know, but I was the one intent on killing the bastard, so when he came after us, as far as I am concerned, I alone pulled the trigger. That is something Zade feels he should have done years ago, and for that, Zade feels ashamed. "

I reach for another glass of mimosa and down it like the first glass. Kyren reaches across and grabs my wrists, turning it so that he can see the faint scars.

"Baby, as far as I am concerned, you did what you had to do for you and your brother to survive, and there is no shame in that for either of you."

But in that instant, I see something sad and haunting in his blue eyes. It passes so quickly, I think I have imagined it. I don't like the pain I see in his eyes. This time, instead of reaching for the glass, I grab the bottle of champagne and drink directly from the bottle.

Kyren throws his head back laughing. "You keep that up, baby, and you will ruin my plans for the evening," he says, grinning at me.

I put the bottle down. Plans? That's sobering. "What do you have in mind?" I put on a seductive smile.

"Not what your obviously thinking, you naughty girl."

"Why not?" I ask, sticking out a playful pouted lip. "A movie. Now we're talking make out time. If you are good, you might get to third base."

"No." He's rolling his eyes at me with a shy grin on his face.

"Oh, you actually want to watch a movie?" I am a little disappointed.

"Yes, I love the *Ironman* movies." He has a hopeful look in his eyes.

"Oh my god, really?" I say laughing. "I didn't peg you for a superhero guy."

"Well, I'm certainly not a chick flick kind of guy." He pretends to be offended.

"All right. On one condition."

"Popcorn?" He is grinning again.

"Popcorn and lots of it." I say nodding. "I will have to go home and change clothes."

"I have a better plan. Let's just stop in town and buy you some clothes. I don't want to run the risk of you changing your mind."

I lean back in my chair to look at him. I think he's serious. "Okay, I have had my eye on the perfect little dress and shoes."

"A woman always needs an excuse for new shoes." He lifts his glass and drinks.

Chapter 11

We head into town and stop by a little dress boutique. As I am trying on my dress, I can hear the shop owner swooning over Kyren. It gets under my skin. Jealousy, I think? I have never been jealous of anyone. I choose that moment to step out of the dressing room.

Kyren, who sits between two women, stands up, and his mouth drops open. My dress is white. The top half is sheer and sleeveless and a V neckline. The silk material underneath barely covers my breasts. From the waist down, it has a flowing skirt that hangs midthigh. My sandals are a coral color that matches the silky sash around my waist.

"*You* look *beautiful*." He slowly enunciated each word.

I think he is drooling. I twirl for him to see my flowing skirt, and when I turn back around, both woman are gone, and I can see a bulge in his now tight jeans. I saunter over to him, hoping like hell it looks sexy and not stupid. Sandals were a good choice. I could never pull this off in heels.

I get nose to nose with him and grab the bulge in his pants. "I think you like this dress a lot."

He groans. "Baby, you keep holding that, and we are never going to make it out of this store. And I'm pretty sure those are cameras pointed right at us."

I lean into his ear and whisper, "That's hot, the thought of someone watching us." I take my tongue and trace his earlobe and bite gently.

Kyren growls, grabs me, and kisses me hard. When he pulls back, I am breathless. "Baby, that's all the show they are going to see. Now go get your things and I will pay."

"What? No, Kyren, you're not paying for me!"

He turns to look at me sternly, "This is not open for discussion!"

I open my mouth to protest and then shut it. Holy crap! He is serious. "Yes, sir."

"Good girl. Now get your ass moving before we miss the movie."

Right now, I could give a shit about the movie. I want to take him back into the dressing room and fuck his brains out. He makes me so damn hot. Never has a man been so commanding to me. I really like it. I have never thought of myself as submissive, but I think I could submit to him. Damn cameras!

We walk in the theater armed with popcorn. "Do I get to pick where we sit?" I ask batting my eyes.

He extends his arms out, "If you insist."

"I do. Follow me." We go to the very top row, right in the middle.

"Any special reason you picked these seats, Ms. Milby?"

"No," I say and bat my eyes again.

The theater is filling up, but only a few people sit near us. “Thank you for the popcorn. And, oh yes, the dress and the shoes. That was very sweet of you.”

“You’re welcome,” he says as he playfully grabs the popcorn away.

“Hey! I don’t share movie popcorn,” I say as I playfully swat at his arm.

“Today, you do. I have spent enough money on you today, and I’m not buying my own popcorn. I wouldn’t want to spoil you too much.” I laugh out loud. “Shhhh,” he says. “But I do love it when you laugh.”

By the time the movie actually starts, we have consumed all of our popcorn. I take a sip of my drink and I hear Kyren opening something. “What are you hiding?” I whisper.

“Nothing,” he says as he stuffs his mouth. I pull his ear hard.

“Okay, okay. It’s M&M’s!”

“Plain chocolate?”

“Of course, chocolate. Is there anything better?” He rolls his eyes at me.

“Share, cowboy.” I hold my hand out, and he gives me just one. I can’t help but giggle at his childish behavior.

The movie is about half over, and Kyren is so entranced in the movie, and I am staring at him. Watching his facial expressions is more entertaining than watching the movie. His hands gripped the armrests. I reach over and place my hand on his thigh. No reaction.

Huh. He really is into the movie. Watching his intensity is hot. I move my hand up and down his thigh and caress his cock. I see him inhale.

Yes! Now I have got his attention.

He reaches into the M&M bag and places a few in his mouth then leans over and kisses me, giving me his candy. Then he looks straight at me, blue eyes to lavender. “Stop,” he whispers. His firm command and the chocolate from his mouth just make me even hotter. He turns and continues to watch the movie.

“I am going to combust right here in this chair,” I whisper to him.

He doesn’t even take his eyes off the movie. He leans in. “They have fire extinguishers for that, and you will be okay.”

I can’t help but laugh and decide to let the man finish his movie in peace.

When we leave the theater, it is raining really hard. Kyren runs to get the truck and pulls up close to keep me dry. He, however, is soaked.

“You look good wet,” I say, eyeing him up and down.

“Do I, Ms. Milby?” He is giving me a devilish look.

Just the way he responds has me all hot and bothered again. “Kyren, take me back to my place. The weather is too bad for the boat, and I have to work tomorrow.”

“How will you get to work if your boat is at my house?”

“I will call a cab.”

"No, you won't. I will take you," he says, frowning at me.

"Does that mean you are spending the night?" I'm hopeful.

"Only if I'm invited." He has that shy smile on his face.

"I don't know," I say teasing him. "You have ignored my needs for the last few hours."

He has a hot look on his face. "Your needs?"

"Yes, my needs," I say it slowly.

"I think I can fully and thoroughly make that up to you, Ms. Milby, when I get you home." His look is smoldering more than I can bear.

We have just crossed the bridge to the island and it's raining cats and dogs.

"Stop! The truck!" I yell out.

"What? Why?" Kyren yells back in confusion as he pulls over by a lone streetlight. As soon as he has stopped, I jump out of the truck and run to the driver's side.

Kyren is staring at me through his window with his mouth wide open. I knock on his window, and he opens it just enough to yell out at me. "What the hell are you doing?"

"Come out here with me!" I'm yelling over the pounding rain.

"Brogan, it's pouring! Have you lost all good sense?"

"A little rain never hurt anyone. Come on, I want to play."

He hesitates then he rolls his window back up. I can hear him grumbling and see him taking off his boots. His door opens, and I grab his hand, not giving him a chance to change his mind.

"Brogan, you ain't right, baby!" he continues to grumble.

I am laughing at him, soaking wet, and climbing into the back of his truck. I stand in the middle of the bed and wait for him to join me. He growls once more then he jumps in and stands right in front of me, staring. I then see his eyes scan my body. My white dress is now see-through. He reaches out and roughly grabs my ass, pulling me into his hard cock.

"No panties, Ms. Milby? If I would have known, we would have been kicked out of the theater for inappropriate behavior."

"You can behave inappropriately now." Every part of me is on fire for him.

"Oh, baby, I plan to." Then his mouth is on me, hard. Our hands are everywhere.

He pushes me toward the cab of the truck. Between gritted teeth, I hear him say, "You have been teasing me for hours, and now I am going to punish you then fuck you," he growls.

I have literally gum busted. Wetness, not from the rain, is running between my legs. He sits on the edge of the truck and takes me with him. Before I even realize what he is doing, he has me bent over his knees and has hiked up the skirt of my dress. Then I feel the smack of his hand on my ass. I yell out from sheer surprise, not pain. Then he smacks me again on the other cheek. I am use to being in charge, but this is really hot! I have never been spanked for pleasure. Two more smacks then he bends me over the truck and I hear the sound of his zipper. He reaches between my legs.

"You are so fucking wet, baby. I'm going to fuck you hard and fast!"

I almost come right then and there. He spreads my legs with his and in on move he thrusts inside me. I scream out in pleasure. He's holding my hip with his left hand and his right hand has reached around to find my nub. He starts to move in fast and out slow. I feel the burning already. I slip and he grabs both my hips and starts moving again. He leans over and bites my ear.

"Touch yourself, baby."

I immediately obey and reach down to rub myself. I can feel his cock going in and out, hard and fast. That's all it takes, and I explode around him, drawing each inward thrust deeper. I hear him growl my name.

"Fuck, Brogan!" Then he stills inside me.

We slide down into the bed of the truck, still joined together. I don't know what comes over me, but I start to laugh. A deep, cathartic laugh. Kyren has pulled out of me and has rolled me over to face him. He is leaning over me shielding my face from the rain. He is grinning, and I feel his laughter building. He rolls off of me, and we are both drenched in the bed of his truck, laughing hysterically.

When the laughter finally fades, he leans back up and kisses me. "Baby, as much as I have enjoyed your crazy antics, we better get you home and out of your wet clothes."

"My wet clothes didn't hamper you a few minutes ago, Mr. Nolan."

He pulls me up and lifts me over his shoulder and smacks my ass again. I yelp and then smack his hard ass back. He laughs and climbs us out of the truck. He opens my door and tosses me inside. I sit up and glance in the rearview mirror. I look a mess, but it didn't seem to bother him one bit. He climbs in the driver's side and is very quiet. The ten-minute drive home is too quiet. He parks the truck outside my house. The rain is now only a drizzle. He just sits there. He makes no move to get out. I can stand the silence no longer. "Kyren, did I do something wrong?"

"Oh god, baby, no. I am just worried." Concern is written all over his face.

"Worried about what?" He has me terrified.

"We have been having sex with no protection. I get so caught up in moments with you that I have completely forgotten to use condoms."

"You had me terrified. You don't have to worry. I'm on the pill. and I'm clean."

I see relief wash over his face. "I'm clean too," he finally says.

"Well, I was clean," I say teasingly.

He turns and looks at me all serious again. "What?"

"I was clean until some madman fucked in me in the bed of his truck."

He grins. "I want to get you inside the house and see if I can get you dirtier."

"Race you," I say, and we are rushing out of the truck and running for the front door. We both head straight for a hot shower, peeling our clothes off as we go.

Chapter 12

The work week goes by quickly. Kyren and I have been texting, or should I say sexting, the last three days. We have both been so busy, we haven't actually seen each other, and I have been taking it out on my kickboxing instructor. Now it's Thursday, and for the first time in years, I cancel my appointment with Dr. Kohl. I feel good. I feel healthy and happy, and I'm desperate to see Kyren. I decide to surprise Kyren at his place. I grab some toys and an overnight bag.

I'm happy that when I arrive, Kyren is not on the yacht. Mrs. Moore lets me in an offers me food.

"Later maybe. Thank you." I am fidgeting

"What is it, dear?" She looks at me curiously.

I'm a little nervous. "Ummmm…I would like to go to Kyren's cabin, but I know he keeps it locked."

"Not a problem, dear." She reaches into one of the cabinets and pulls out a key and hands it to me.

"Thanks," I say shyly. "I'm sure I'm a bright shade of red."

As I make my way down to his bedroom, I get a whiff of that same nauseating cologne again. It takes my breath away. Either his uncle or his client must have been down here. I shake off that eerie feeling and continue on my mission.

I slip into a sexy nightgown and pull out my toys, handcuffs, cat-o'-nine, and a gag ball. Yep these will work perfectly. I then text Kyren with a picture of me in his bed and an invitation to join me. I get a quick response. "I will be there in two minutes. Don't move an inch." I smile and in exactly two minutes he walks through his bedroom door. His look is totally scorching.

"I have missed you," he says as he strides toward me.

"Me too."

He looks at the items I have placed on the bed. "Are these for me to use on you?" His eyebrows are raised, and I think he is smirking at me.

"No." I bite my lower lip waiting for his response.

"Oh," he says and grabs my wrists. "You know you don't need these things, Brogan. I am more than willing and able to meet your needs."

"I know, and you have demonstrated that many times."

"Brogan, you know I like control." He's frowning.

"And so do I."

He tilts his head and locks his blue eyes with mine. He inhales deeply. "I will let you control tonight, if the next time, you let me have complete control over you whatever *I* want."

Damn it. He makes me wet. That sounds like a deal I can handle because I know he likes it rough too. "Deal."

I lean in to kiss him, but he pulls away to look at me. "Wait. Why aren't at Dr. Kohl's office?"

"Because for the first time in my life, I'm okay."

"Are you sure it's a good idea to cancel with Zade coming to town?"

"Zade isn't due here for another week. I will keep my appointment next week. I swear."

He pulls me in for a strong hug. "Okay."

"Now, Mr. Nolan, take your clothes off. I have been dying to get my hands on you."

He quickly obeys and is standing in front of me with a beautiful hard on.

I reach down and grab the gag. "Have you ever used one of these before?"

"No, but I know what it is."

I reach up and place it in his mouth and attach it around his neck, making sure it is not too tight. "It's to mask your screams." I see him inhale deeply. I stand in front of him and slowly remove my nightgown. He reaches to touch me and a swat him with the cat-o'-nine. "No touching me. I'm not ready to handcuff you yet."

He stills, and I walk around him kissing his body as I go. I bite his shoulder, and I hear his inhale and moan.

"I want you to stroke your cock." He obediently slides his hand down his body to stroke himself. I join my hand with his. He is stroking long and hard. I walk around to the front of him and get on my knees. I slowly lick the tip of his cock. His hands immediately grab my hair.

I stop and stand up and snatch the handcuffs off the bed. "Hands behind your back," I command. I see his cock spasm and grow bigger.

He willingly complies. "I have one more surprise for you." I reach in my bag and pull out a cock ring. I slowly roll it onto his length and the look on his face makes me spasm and drench with wetness. I return to my knees and take him back in my mouth and firmly suck his shaft. I hear him groan behind the gag. I firmly push him backward until he is sitting on the bed.

I begin my relentless sucking in and out, and I can still feel him growing. The ring is preventing him from coming. He is on his elbows hands remain cuffed behind his back. I hear his muffled pleas, and sweat is beading off of him. I continue until I feel he can take no more. I roll off the ring, and as I do, his hips buck off the bed, and there is a muffled, animalistic scream. He comes hotly and hard into my mouth. His head falls to the bed, and his chest is heaving. I am so not done with him. I climb up his body and lightly swat him on the chest and abs with the cat-o'-nine. His eyes fly open, and they are the color of a storm. He tries to push himself up, but I firmly place my hand on his chest. He is staring into my lavender eyes, and the heat coming off him makes me ache deep inside. I reach up and unhook his gag.

An exhaled rasp leaves his lungs. "Please, Brogan…" It's a deep husky sexy sound. I swat him again. "No talking," I say sternly. Then I kiss him deeply. As our lips part, I whisper, "Roll over." I get up on my hands and knees, allowing him room to maneuver. He rolls, and I unlock his handcuffs. I slowly rub his arms, wrists, and shoulders. I move down his back to massage him, including his scars. He stills for a moment as I lean down and kiss each scar. I can see him visibly relaxing. I kiss him from his neck all the way to his perfect ass. He rolls over and I let him.

His cock is already thick and hard again. I lean over and plant a kiss on the tip of it, and before I can even react, he has flipped me over, pulled me up the bed, and has pinned me with his body. We wrestle for control before I give in because he is so much stronger. It is useless.

We are staring at each other, blue to lavender. While holding my wrist above my head with his left hand, his right hand grabs my left breast and squeezes firmly. Then his teeth are pulling at my nipple. He is relentless, and I automatically start moving my hips. As I do, he clenches down on my nipple hard, and it's painful but followed by pure pleasure. I explode. I have never had an orgasm from a man pleasuring my nipples before. It is quick and hard and leaves me wanting for more.

He has made his way between my thighs and is kissing and sucking on that sweet spot. I come again, and as soon as I start, he has grabbed me so that I am sitting on him, nose to nose, and he impales himself deep inside me. I scream out his name. He is pumping in and out of me as I continue to come apart around him.

As I am coming down, I hear him say, "Fuck! Oh, fuck!" Then he pushes deeper inside, and I feel his sweet release. We collapse back onto the bed, but he remains inside me. I hear him talking, but I'm so exhausted and satiated, I can't make out what he is saying.

"Brogan!" he snaps as he rolls off of me. "Look at me!" he commands. My eyes flutter open. "I was really rough. Did I hurt you?" He looks painfully sincere.

I try to regain my composure. "Well, it hurt a little, but in a good way, and in a way I wanted to be hurt." I brush his cheek.

"Baby, I'm sorry. I got carried away." He is rubbing his hands through his hair.

I roll to my side and grab his chin. "Kyren, look at me," I mimic his earlier words. "I loved every minute of what we just did. There is nothing for you to be sorry about. Except, well…"

He looks alarmed. "Well, what?"

"I thought I was the one in control. Somehow, you took over," I say, smiling at him.

"A man can only stand so much," he says playfully. "You were driving me mad." He swats me on the ass. "Besides, whether you admit it or not, I think you like it when I take control."

"Only with you, baby," I say as I touch his beautiful face.

I lay quietly in his embrace, which is no longer awkward for me.

"How was your day?" I ask him quietly.

"Good. Plans are moving right along. We should be finished soon."

"Was your client in here today?"

"Yes, why?"

"I could smell that nasty cologne, and I know your uncle doesn't usually step foot on your boat."

"He was wanting to see the size of my closet. He is wanting to make a few adjustments to his."

"I know it's weird because I have never met him, but I just don't like him."

"He is kind of odd. Seems to be a loner. Makes me wonder why he needs a yacht. He doesn't strike me as the kind of guy who entertains."

"Are you ever going to tell me about your scars?"

"Whoa, change of subject," he says, smiling. "I will. I promise. But right now, I need food. You have drained me of all my energy. I worked hard all day and then got laid by a beautiful auburn-haired girl as soon as I walked in the door."

"Girl!" I roll on top of him. "Have I not just proven to you that I am all woman?" I ask as I stroke my tongue on his chin.

He laughs. "Oh, baby, you are enough woman for ten men."

"Only ten?" I ask, smirking at him.

He abruptly sits up, and we are face to face. "I am the only man you need, and I will meet all your needs and some that you don't even know you have. No other men. Do you understand?" For a moment, his possessiveness frightens me. I just stare at him. "I don't share." His face is so stern.

I let out my breath that I didn't realize I was holding. "Good. I don't want to be shared, but the same goes for you."

His face looks relieved. "Agreed. Now get your naked ass off of me so that I can consume large amounts of food so that I can take care of my woman."

I climb out of bed, laughing, and head straight to the bathroom to clean up. His woman. The thought doesn't scare me; it brings warmth to my once cold soul. I think about how quickly he has changed my life and became part of my heart. I never thought I would feel this comfortable with another soul.

He steps in the bathroom and interrupts my thoughts. “Hey, beautiful. Let’s go eat.”

We spend the rest of the evening eating, drinking wine, and laughing at each other’s stories. Normal. Just plain normal. It was completely awesome. We curl up in front of the fireplace and Kyren is reading aloud a book on the history of boats. He is very excited as he reads, but I can’t help nodding off a few times. I wake to Kyren lifting me in his arms and carrying me to bed. I curl into his strong arms. He gently sets me down on the edge of the bed. “Arms up, sleepyhead,” he says and he undresses me until I am completely naked. I look awkwardly up at him.

“No. No sex. I just don’t want anything between us when we sleep. Now lay down.”

He quickly rids himself of his clothes, climbs into bed next to me, my back to his front. He covers us up and pulls me in tight. I am already drifting off to sleep again when I hear him say, “Good night, Brogan,” and then he kisses the top of my head.

My hand is shaking, but I aim and squeeze the trigger. A blood curdling scream and down he went, cursing before he hit the ground with a thud.

“Untie me, Brogan.” I scramble over to Zade and fumble with the knots in the rope. Finally, Zade is free. I turn to see movement.

My father is up and coming straight for us. "Give me the gun Brogan! No!" I scream. "Back!" Zade grabs the gun with me and pulls the trigger.

"Wake up, Brogan. Wake up!"

I gasp and sit straight up. Kyren is sitting on the edge of the bed, wide-eyed. I am shaking and sweating profusely. "It's okay. You're okay. It was just a bad dream," he says as he pulls me into his arms. We sit there, silently holding each other for a while. Finally, Kyren breaks the silence. "You didn't see Dr. Kohl this week." It is a statement not a question. "Do you think that is why the nightmares are back? Just a thought."

Something triggered it. Maybe it was the smell of that man's cologne. "I don't know. Things have been so good lately, I just thought I could manage on my own."

"I think you are better, but Zade is coming to town, and Cady has been gone, and I think you are worried about Zade. Maybe you should try to see Dr. Kohl today."

"Okay. It is three in morning. I will call him in the morning. Can you please just hold me for now?"

He holds me, but I keep fidgeting. I can't shake the fear of my nightmare. Then I hear him whisper so softly that I thought I was dreaming. "The beating that left me scarred didn't hurt me. I was numb." I try to rollover to face him. "No," he whispers. "I want to tell you the story, but I can't bear the thought of you looking at me."

"Whatever it is, Kyren, I won't judge you."

"I know, but you might leave me, and that would tear me apart."

"I won't leave you, but if that is your fear, then don't tell me baby. But I cannot imagine that it is worse than me telling you that I killed my own father and you didn't leave me."

He is quiet for a minute before he starts again. He's holding me tight as to prevent me from leaving or security, I'm not sure which. "I joined the military when the towers went down. I was sent overseas to Afghanistan. I was just a kid but felt the need to defend our country. My troop was traveling by Humvees when we were ambushed. My buddy Joe and I were the only ones that survived, and we were captured." He draws a long breath in, and I find myself softly touching his face. I can feel unshed tears in his stormy blue eyes. "Joe was badly injured and was bleeding profusely from one of his legs, which was barely hanging on. They brutally drug us to a nearby cave. They tortured Joe by cutting off what was left of his leg."

I gasped and tears are now flowing down my face. Kyren takes another deep inhale, shuts his eyes tight, and continues. "It was the most godawful sound. He screamed until he passed out."

I feel Kyren shudder against me, but I remain silent, willing him to go on.

"They had me stripped of my clothes and tied me to a post that had obviously been used to torture others. My back was to them, and Joe lay beside me. I prayed that he was dead, so they couldn't hurt him anymore. I could hear them talking amongst themselves, but they had yet to torture me. I kept bracing myself for it but nothing.

"After about an hour or so, I saw Joe moving. He was alive but in agony. It was then that I felt the crack of the whip across my back, but I refused to yell out in pain. One of their men came over to Joe and picked him up by his hair and pulled him in front of me. Joe had tears streaming down his dirt-smudged face. His eyes were burning into me, begging me for something.

"'If you get out of this alive, tell my wife and daughter I love them, but to go on with their lives and be happy.' It was all Joe could get out. 'No! We are leaving together one way or another,' I told him." Kyren is silent.

"Kyren," I whispered, "what happened next?"

Kyren breathed in really deep and exhaled. "I was a stupid kid. I didn't realize my words would only antagonize my enemies."

"Go on," I encouraged him, not realizing my own tears flowing down my cheeks. He leaned his head to mine, and that's when I felt his tears.

"The one that was holding up Joe laughed then said, 'You two have a choice to make. One of you will live. The other will die here in this cave. Which one is your choice?' He said it with his haunting laugh."

Oh my god, no! "What?"

"He made us choose." Kyren hangs his head in shame. Oh this can't be good. He may be more broken than me. I can feel his pain coming off of him. "I begged them to kill me. Joe had a family. Joe screamed over me to kill him. He kept saying he was dead anyway. There was no way he would make it out alive. He had lost too much blood and would never make it back to base. 'You can live, Kyren, and you will survive,' he just kept screaming it. 'Okay, boys, which one shall it be? You have to be in agreement or I will personally torture you both to the brink of death and bring you back for more over and over,'" he said. Joe screamed, 'Me. Kill me!'

"'No. No, Joe! I can't!' And as the words left my mouth. I felt the crack of the whip through my back. Then the whip was digging into Joe's face.

"'God, please, Kyren. Let me die,' Joe whimpered. Another lash across my back. I couldn't feel my pain, only Joe's.

"'I will ask again, boys. Who will it be?" The bastard was smiling.

"'Please, Kyren, I'm begging you. Kill me!' Joe screams with every ounce of breath left in his body.

"Our enemy just stare at me, laughing. 'Your answer, boy?'

"My head is hung, and I cannot bear to look at Joe. Tears are rolling down my face, not from the physical pain of the whip, but the pain of my decision. I barely whisper his name, 'Joe.'

"'What, boy?' Our enemy yells and kicks what remains of Joe's leg. Joe cries in agony.

"'Joe!' I scream. May God forgive me. Without hesitation, the man lifts his gun to Joe's head and pulls the trigger."

"No!" I scream out loud at Kyren. Kyren pulls me in tighter, and I can feel his gut-wrenching sobs.

"Oh my god, Kyren. I am so sorry, baby." I lie with Kyren until I feel his chest stop heaving.

"After they killed him, they continued to beat me with the whip over and over. I just wanted to die. When I wouldn't scream out in pain, they gave up. They released me. They took Joe's body and left. I lay in that cave for maybe a day before I could face getting up. They weren't coming back to finish me off. The only thing that finally brought me back to my feet that day was Joe's words about his family. I had to make it back to deliver his message to his family and let them know that Joe was a hero."

"Did you deliver his message?"

"It took me awhile to heal and to get over the guilt, but one year later, I did. I told his wife everything that happened. She slapped me. She told me she would never forgive me for allowing him to die instead of me. I should have fought harder. I went in the military to be a hero; instead, I left a coward."

"No, Kyren, you did fight and you survived like Joe wanted you to."

Kyren's head is bent on his folded hands. "Maybe she was right. I felt so guilty. I drank a lot, ignored my life, my girlfriend. I put myself into these yachts."

"And now Kyren?"

"I still feel some guilt, but I have tried hard."

"How?"

"At first, I lived with Uncle Tom when I started building yachts. I had no idea how successful I would be. Every extra dime I made, I sent to Joe's family. I was determined to take care of them financially and have them want for nothing. I guess I owe not only my life but my success to Joe. Joe's wife and daughter are well taken care of for the rest of their lives."

"And his wife? Did you ever see her again?"

"Yes, four years ago. She tracked me down. She told me she was grateful for me taking care of them. She said she was sorry for the things she had said to me that day. She knew what kind of man Joe was, and he made the right decision. Joe would have died anyways. She told me I needed to let go of the guilt and forgive myself. She had since moved on and is happy."

"Do you still send her money?"

"Not his wife. She asked me not to send any more money. That I had done enough. It was time to let go."

"But?"

"Every year, I deposit money into his daughters account."

"You are a good man, Kyren. How could you ever think I could ever leave you over your heartache?"

"For fuck's sake, Brogan. I killed a man!"

I forcefully disengage from Kyren's embrace and push him down on the bed and sit on top of him. "Look at me, Kyren! Joe made a choice. He would not have survived. You both knew it. You didn't kill him. He saved your life, and you in turn saved his family. You are not a coward. You were both brave men. You did not pull the trigger by saying his name. Joe was a hero. Don't take that away from him by laying claim to killing him."

I can see in the dim light coming in from the moon and peeping through the curtains that Kyren has tears running down his face. I gently lean down and start kissing his tears away. Before I can stop myself, I say, “I am madly in love with you Kyren.”

He stills then gently kisses my lips. “I love you too, Brogan. I fell in love with you the moment I laid eyes on you.”

We both lie there in each other’s arms until we both drifted off to sleep.

Chapter 13

When I woke the next morning, Kyren was already gone. He left me a note on his pillow. It simply said, "Have a good day, baby. I. Love. You."

I smile and head for the shower. As I am washing, I recall Kyren's story. He is amazing, and I am so glad he finally told me his story. I feel very connected to him and very protective. I found myself kind of angry with Joe's wife for how see treated him. He had found the courage to tell her the truth, no matter how bad it was. Kyren has punished himself enough. His keeping his scars is a reminder of his guilt to Joe. Now I wish we could fully remove them for him.

I quickly finish my shower. As I'm dressing, I decide to call Dr. Kohl's office. Ann mumbles something about me missing my appointment but agrees to fit me in an hour.

As I dock the boat, I grab my phone and call Cady.

"Hey, Brogan. I've missed you," she yells into the phone.

"I've missed you too. When are you coming home?"

"Next week when Zade gets in. Why? What's wrong?" I can hear the concern in her voice.

"I told Kyren I loved him."

Then I hear this high-pitch scream, "Oh, Brogan. That's the greatest news, sweetie. I'm so happy for you…Wait…Did he say it back?" she says a little softer.

"Yes."

"That's great! But you are scared, aren't you?"

"Oddly enough, no. I'm…I'm…happy."

"I didn't think I would ever hear you say that about a man."

I can't help but giggle. "I know, right?"

I can hear Cady's excitement in the phone. I can just picture her doing some kind of happy dance. "I'm so happy for you. I can hardly wait to meet Kyren. We can all go out and celebrate when I get home."

I am all caught up in her excitement. "I can't wait for you to meet him. You're going to love him."

We catch up for a few more minutes then I head to Dr. Kohl's office feeling utterly happy. Ann has an annoyed look on her face and points to the door to go in. Dr. Kohl is already sitting in his usual chair. His smile is warm when he sees me.

"Good morning, Brogan. I'm glad you are here. I always worry when someone I have been seeing for years cancels on me." He smiles, but I can see the worry etched on his face.

"I'm sorry, Dr. Kohl. I thought I could skip out on you just once. I thought I could handle things without you."

"Has something happened in a day that has changed your mind?" He is leaning forward on his knees.

I break out into a big smile. "I've been good, I mean really good and…happy for the first time since…well, the first time I can remember. No pills, no nightmares, and a man I am crazy in love with."

Dr. Kohl sits straight in his chair, and I think he is smirking at me. "Love? Well, that is progress."

I proceed to tell him all about Kyren, including the story of his scars, knowing very well that Dr. Kohl can't repeat it.

"It sounds like the two of you have some of the same demons. So I'm curious. What made you come in today?"

"Well, I lied about the no-nightmare thing," I say guiltily. "I had another nightmare last night. Same one but very vivid."

"And you want me to tell you why." It is a statement, not a question.

"Yes, you are the shrink. Shrink me," I say, waving my hands in the air.

Dr. Kohl laughs. "You know, it doesn't work that way, Brogan."

I get up from the chair and start my usual pacing. "Well, what the hell, Dr. Kohl? Help a girl out. Tell me something."

"Please quit pacing and sit back down. What were you doing?"

"Ah, sleeping. Duh."

"Your sarcasm is not helping," he says frustrated. "Did something happen to you during the day to trigger it? Did Kyren whisper sweet nothings in your ear, Brogan?" he says, grinning.

"Now whose sarcasm isn't helping?" I ask, scowling at him with my arms folded across my chest.

"Okay, truce. I'm sorry, Brogan, that was very unprofessional of me. But was there a trigger?"

I sit back and relax and think about what he is asking me. "A smell."

"A smell?"

"Cologne like my father used to wear."

"A smell can bring about very strong emotional trigger. I suggest you simply ask Kyren not to wear it anymore. I am sure he will understand."

"It wasn't his. He is building a boat…um, yacht for a man, and he had been in Kyren's yacht, and the smell lingered."

"Did you meet him?"

"No. He is Kyren's client."

"I think you should meet him."

"Why?" I ask confused.

"So you can associate that scent with something other than your father's. So that it will no longer be a trigger for you.

"Oh, okay. That makes sense, I guess. I will ask Kyren to set up an introduction." I sit still and silent for a minute.

"Is there something else, Brogan?"

"How is he really?"

I don't have to clarify who the he is. "Zade is really good and excited about seeing you."

"You mean anxious and scared."

"No, Brogan. Excited," he says as he leans forward again in his chair, but this time, he locks his eyes with mine. "He wants a good healthy relationship with you. He has reclaimed his life. and that life involves the sister he loves and adores. Can you give him that. Brogan?"

"I so badly want to, I guess. I'm the one who is really anxious and scared."

"I know you are, but Zade is really, really good and healthy. And, well, just look at you, you are by your own admission…happy."

I smile and let his words sink in. "Yes. Yes, I am. Thank you, Dr. Kohl. I know I have given you a hard time over the years, but I am truly thankful for the progress you have made with Zade."

"And what about with you, Brogan?"

"I'm better. Still broken but better."

He sits back in his chair and frowns.

"Thank you for me too, Dr. Kohl," and then I do something totally out of character, I get up from my chair. Dr. Kohl rises as well. I walk up to him and put my arms around him in a hug. I think he is stunned because he takes a few seconds before he returns my hug. "You are the closest thing that Zade and I have had for a father, and I love you for that." I squeeze him one last time, and when I let go, I see the wetness in Dr. Kohl's eyes.

He clears his throat and simply states, "You are no longer broken," and he pats my cheek.

I leave Dr. Kohl's office and head straight for the gym. I am feeling so energized. For the first time, I am looking forward to seeing Zade. I have really missed him. The phone rings and breaks my thoughts. It's Kyren, and I find myself smiling like a school girl.

“Hey, baby,” he growls in that sexy tone. I just keep grinning.

“There is a concert Saturday night where we first met. Even though not all the memories are good from then, it is where my life changed, and I want us to go.”

“It would be my pleasure, sir, but you might want to wear some protection just in case I want to relive the memories.”

He chuckles. “Duly noted.” Then he proceeds to tell me that we can’t hang out the next day.

“I am a little disappointed, but I have been dying to curl up with a good book and get lost in someone else’s fantasy.”

“Replaced by a book already,” he says, teasing me.

“Never. The pages can’t keep me warm. Horny but not warm.”

“Ahh, I see. You are reading smut.” I can hear him smiling.

“How else do you think I learn ways to blow your mind?”

“It wasn’t my mind I was thinking about you blowing,” he says, huskily.

Now I am laughing at him. “You are as bad as me, and I love it, but now you have me all horny just with your sexy voice, and your leaving me all alone tonight. But I love you anyway.”

“I love you too, baby. Now tell me all about your day.”

I tell him all about my meeting with Dr. Kohl and his suggestion to meet his client.

“I can arrange that for you next week. He is out of town for a few days.”

“Okay. No rush. At least his cologne won’t be lingering around.”

“Go curl up with that book of yours, baby, so we can practice all your new tricks you have learned tomorrow.”

“Good night, Kyren,” I say softly.

“Brogan?”

“What?”

“Tomorrow night is my way, remember? I get to have you however I want you, and I will be in complete control.”

“I remember, and I am wet just thinking about it.”

“Good night, Brogan,” he says with what I think is a smile on his handsome face.

Chapter 14

The band that is playing on the dock tonight is a country band, so I decide to buy me a new pair of boots for the occasion. The boots lead to new shorts and a hat. My shorts are very short and fit my ass nicely. I also bought a white wifebeater top like what Kyren wears. I slip on a long silver necklace that dangles over my breast. It has a silver ball with tassels at the end, so every time I move, it sways. My boots are black and entwined with brown. Big dangling earrings finish off my outfit. My hair is off my right shoulder in a messy fishtail braid. I place my hat on my head as I look in the mirror. This should do just fine, but my thoughts go primal. I immediately think about getting a rope and lassoing Kyren then I remember it's his night to be in control. I can't help but hope that whatever he has planned, it is kinky as hell. Damn it! I'm wet again.

Kyren is on time as usual. When I open the door, his eyes pop out of his head. He growls, "You look good, cowgirl, and I don't ever want you to remove those boots." His look alone has me gushing.

"They will be even better around your ears," I say seductively.

He grabs me and gives me a heated kiss. He nips at my neck. "Keep this up, and we won't make it to see the band."

"I'm good with that. We can fuck right here, right now," I say as I grab his already hard cock through his jeans.

"I love your dirty mouth and mind and especially your eager hands, but I'm in control tonight. That is the plan," he states as he removes my hand and gives it a squeeze.

"Please, I'm not beyond begging," I say, whimpering.

"You are an insatiable woman, but don't worry, I promise you *will* be satiated later.

I am a pile of wetness in his arms, but how can I deny him what he wants. I unwilling step out of his arms. My brain makes me move, but my body has a hard time following. I pout, and he breaks out in a breathtaking smile. He kisses me lightly, grabs my hand, and leads me out the door.

"Your ass looks very tempting in those tight jeans of yours, Mr. Nolan," I say as a swat him on that hot ass.

"I'm glad you are enjoying the view, Ms. Milby, but flattery and flirting will not get me back inside the house."

"Who needs the house? The driveway is looking pretty good to me."

He grabs me again and kisses me hard. I think I have won because I can feel his erection jabbing into my hip. He slaps my ass hard. "In the truck, now. And no, not for fucking." He is gritting his teeth in restraint. I do as he says, but totally disappointed and soaking wet. It is a beautiful night. White lights are flickering all over the dock. This is the first time I have had a date for one of these events, and I am getting some strange stares. I am feeling a little shy under watchful eyes. Kyren grabs my hand, getting my attention.

"Let's dance." It is a slow song, and I willingly return Kyren's embrace as we dance.

"Everyone is staring," I whisper to Kyren.

"That's because you look hot in those boots," he whispers and nips my ear.

"And maybe the fact that your hands are all over my ass."

"Where else would you like my hands to be, Ms. Milby?"

I nip back at his ear, "I could think of a few different places," I say seductively.

"Well then, Ms. Milby, not only would they be staring, they would be having us arrested for indecent exposure," he says, laughing.

"Yes. In this small town, you are right," I say, and I am giggling. Me giggling. What in the hell is wrong with me?

"I like hearing you giggle," he says as he leans in and kisses my forehead.

We continue to dance, and over his shoulder, I see Dr. Kohl. He waves, and I drag Kyren over to meet him. "Dr. Kohl, this is Kyren."

"It is so nice to meet the man that is making Brogan so happy."

"I feel the same way, Dr. Kohl. It is my pleasure to meet you."

They shake hands and chat casually for a few minutes, and then Dr. Kohl asks if I would get him a drink?

I hesitate and Kyren softly leans in and says it's okay. "Get me a beer while you are there, wench." He playfully slaps me on the ass and gently pushes me toward the bar.

Why am I so hesitant? Kyren knows my story and Dr. Kohl would never disclose anything anyway. The line is long and I really want to get back, but I wait patiently. Ten minutes later, I walk up to them both with their drinks, and the bastards grab their drinks and wink at me.

“Thanks,” Dr. Kohl says. “I see a pretty girl I would like to dance with. You two have a nice evening. It was nice meeting you, Kyren.”

“Thank you, you too.” They shake hands again.

Kyren gulps down his beer and takes me back to the dance floor. For some reason, I am not quite as comfortable in his embrace. Kyren senses it and pulls me closer.

“What is it, Brogan?”

“Did he tell you how broken I really am?” I ask softly, looking into his pale blue eyes.

“Broken beyond repair,” he says, grinning at me.

“Not funny, Kyren.” I pout for real.

“No, he didn’t tell me you’re broken. Even if he did, I already knew that.”

He is teasing me again, I think. Bastard!

“He told me I have done more for you in a few weeks that he has been able to accomplish in years of work with you. He just wanted to thank me for being in your life.”

“Thank you? I am a little confused.”

“He thinks of you as daughter, Brogan, and he is glad to see you happy and in love.”

“He said that?” I soften.

“Yes, he did.”

“Wow. I knew I thought of him as a father figure, but I didn’t realize he thought of me as a daughter. I just thought he was doing his job. He must be sorry and disappointed. He got the short end of the stick.”

Kyren grabs me by the shoulders, “No, Brogan, he is not disappointed. He is very proud of you.”

No one has ever been proud of me. It is a strange feeling. “It’s nice to hear,” I say flatly. Changing the subject, I ask, “What are your expectations of me tonight…,” I add, “sir?” for effect. I purposely bite my lip.

“My first plan is to sweep you off your feet.”

“Well, that was done in my doorway, so check that off your plan.” I love him playful.

“The rest, Ms. Milby, is a surprise.”

Just the thought makes me ache for him. “Well, whatever your master plan is, can you be quick about it because your hips swaying with mine has created a deep need,” I say as I rock my hips harder into his groin.

I see him bite the inside of his cheeks. Just the effect I wanted. “Ahhh, Ms. Milby. You keep forgetting that I am in charge tonight.” He grabs my hips and pushes his erection right where I want it so badly.

I groan. “I think that bulge in your pants puts me in charge, Mr. Nolan.”

He leans into my ear, "My cock does have a mind of its own, but I can reassure you that I am fully in control."

Holy fuck! I am going to combust right here on this dance floor. and I don't give a fuck who is staring.

"Now you will be a good girl and behave," he says and he leans in and tugs at my lip with his teeth. The bastard knows my reaction to him. I try to bite him back, but he pulls me away. "Let's mingle a little and go get some ice cream from my aunt."

"Okay, but no vanilla," I say, teasing him back.

"Vanilla can be very sweet, Ms. Milby. Don't ditch it until you have tried it."

"No, thank you," I say as I lock with his arm.

We order our ice cream and sit on the edge of the dock, swinging our legs like children. Kyren has been very quiet since the dance floor.

"What's eating you, Kyren?"

"Just a little nervous," he says shyly.

"Nervous about what?" I ask, frowning in concern.

"You," and his eyes are serious and scaring me.

"Me? Why?" I am completely dumbfounded.

"About tonight." He is now looking down at his hands.

I wrap by arm in his, "You mean step two?"

"Yes."

Now I really don't want to wait any longer. "I love you, Kyren. I know, whatever you have planned, you will take care of me and know so well what I like. You have come to know my body better than I do."

"Yes, I do, and I need you to trust me completely." His now dark blue eyes are so serious.

"I do," I say softly. Now he has my mind reeling. What could he have planned that he thinks I wouldn't trust him? The rougher the better. Maybe he's afraid of hurting me?

I get up and reach for his hand. "Come, cowboy. I am more than ready, willing, and impatiently waiting for step two."

Chapter 15

We return to my house, and I see candles flickering on the inside. I jump out of the truck and run to open the door. There are candles everywhere and soft music crooning. I turn to find Kyren standing hesitantly in the doorway.

"What the heck? Who?

"Uncle Tom. I hope you don't mind. You never lock your door, which you should, by the way."

I'm whispering and walking toward him. "No. No, it's okay. It's…beautiful."

He walks over to a bottle of wine that has been chilling. He opens it and pours two glasses. "This is really romantic, Kyren. It is a little too sweet and romantic for me." Then it dawns on me why he is so nervous. I take a big gulp of wine that he has handed me. "This is the second step," he says, and it is almost in a whisper.

He steps closer to me like approaching a scared child. He reaches softly and rubs my cheek. It makes me almost flinch. I have to remind myself of who is touching me.

"I want to make love to you, Brogan."

"You frightened me for a minute there. Make love we can do, and we do often." I relax a little.

"No, Brogan. We fuck. I want to make slow, tender love to you." His eyes show concern.

I finish the rest of my wine in one gulp. It burns, but I needed the pain. I have involuntarily stepped back from him. I can feel my nerves standing on end.

"But why?" I say a little too forcefully.

He steps forward. "Because I want you to completely trust me, Brogan."

I step back. "You want vanilla?"

He steps forward again and now has me pinned to the wall. He lifts his hand to touch my jawline. "I want to touch you tenderly without you flinching."

"Kyren…you know how broken I am. I can't." I stepped around him, and I'm now pacing.

He comes up behind me and grabs me by the hips to still me. "We can, Brogan. I love you, and I want to show you that tenderness can be good too."

His words have terrified me. I thought I could do anything with this man. He turns me and holds out his hand. He is silently asking my permission for his trust. Our eyes are locked. Can I really do this? I love him. I take in a deep breath and slowly put my hand in his. I do trust him. I am scared to death, but this is what he needs from me, and maybe it is what I need too. My heart knows it, but my head wants to put the brakes on.

He takes my hand in his and takes a step, but I don't move with him. "Brogan baby, it's okay. Please trust me." It's a plea.

My heart wins out, and I take a step with him. He picks up pace, probably so that I don't have time to think and change my mind. We reach the bedroom. It is also littered with candles. He stops in front of the bed. We are now face to face. I wonder if he sees my fear.

"I want to undress you," he says quietly.

I start to lift my shirt, and his hands halted my progress. "No, baby, I want to undress you. Let me, please."

"Okay," I say shyly.

"Sit on the bed," he commands, "so I can take your boots off."

"But I thought—"

"Hush, Brogan. I'm in charge." I purse my lips together. He squats in front of me and places his hands on my thighs. He softly caresses my legs. I can feel beads of sweat forming on my body, but at the same time, I have goosebumps. He continues. He slides both his hands down and agonizingly, slowly, gently removes my boots. It is all I can do to sit still. My lip hurts from biting down too hard. He reaches up and gently pulls off my top. He leaves on my lacey nude-colored bra. He rubs his hands softly over my arms. He wraps one arm around my neck and tenderly draws me into a soft, sensual kiss. Gentle passion. He kisses my chin and licks his way to my neck to that delicious spot below my ear. It is then that I realize that I am wet. Even though his touches are gentle, I want him. I need him inside me. I quickly wrap my arms around him and start kissing him hard. He breaks free, breathing hard.

"No, Brogan," he huffs out. "Let me take you there. Let me make love to you."

It's another plea from him. A plea to trust. I let go and let him continue with his gentle touch and exploration of my body. He stands me up and slides his hands down to unbutton my shorts. I am left standing in my bra and thin next-to-nothing panties. He steps back and removes his boots.

"I want you to undress me just as tenderly as I undressed you." Our eyes remain locked. I shakily step forward and slowly reach for the hem of his shirt. His skin feels like it is on fire. I feel another gust of moister between my thighs. I slowly walk behind him, kissing his shoulders, resisting the urge to bite him. I kiss his scars and reach around him for the fly on his jeans. I slowly unzip them and remove his jeans and boxers together. When I walk around to face him, his cock is larger and harder than I have ever seen it. I can't help but smile.

"Are you enjoying yourself, Brogan?" There is so much heat in his tone.

"Yes," I whisper.

He returns to gently kissing and licking me, all the while removing my bra and panties. His eyes lock with mine again, and his body gently nudges me until I can feel the bed behind me. He lays me down, but he remains standing.

"You are beautiful. Perfect." I close my eyes and turn my head, not wanting to hear his words.

"Brogan, look at me." I shake my head. He commands again, "Brogan, look at me now and don't take your eyes off of me." I slowly unclench my eyes and I see heat and tenderness in his eyes.

"Trust me, baby." I watch as he crawls between my legs. He kisses my inner thighs, whispering between each kiss, "You are beautiful. I want you so badly. I love you." All the while, he is looking at me. It's very erotic. I then watch as his head finally dips between my legs.

Our eyes are still locked and watching him kiss and gentle suck me brings on an unexpected orgasm. My hips bolt upward, and his hands push me back down, and he is still fucking looking at me. Once my orgasm ends, he crawls up my body, kissing it as he goes. He stops on my breasts. His hands make contact, and I nearly come again. He kneads them and lightly pinches my nipples. Then his hands are on my neck. His eyes find mine again, and we are nose to nose. He kisses me softly on the lips. I feel his legs nudging my legs apart. When he has me where he wants me, he raises up, and grabs his cock. I can see a drop of dew on the tip, and I can tell he is fighting for his own control. He gently places the tip just barely inside me. I shudder in anticipation, not fear.

"You are so wet, baby. So ready for me."

"Yes," I say, breathless.

He slowly pushes into me. He is so fucking hard. Now I'm the one fighting for control. I can feel my body start to squeeze around him.

He freezes. "Fuck!" he blurts out. I feel him trembling. "Give me a minute," he says through gritted teeth.

I remain very still because, god help me, I want him to continue. I don't want to ruin this moment between us.

He blows his breath out a few times. “Okay, baby. Slow.” He slowly pulls almost all the way out and then slowly pushes back into me. He repeats this several times. It is driving me crazy. “Please,” I beg. I’m not sure if I’m begging him to stop, go faster, go slower, I just know I need release.

He then picks up the pace, but he is still gentle. “How close are you, baby?” he growls out.

“Close,” is all I can say.

“What do you need? Because, baby, I am more than close.”

“Just touch me.” But before he can maneuver his hands between us, he shifts his hips, and his cock hits that glorious place deep inside me, and that is all it takes. I explode in one of the strongest orgasms I have ever had. I hear his animalistic growl and feel his release, which seems hotter and wetter than normal.

When I return to earth, Kyren is lying on top of me, still inside me. He is wringing wet, and so am I. I lay there quietly listening as his breathing calms.

“That was beautiful, Kyren. Like nothing I have ever felt.”

He rolls off of me, taking me with him, but not breaking our precious connection. “Thank you for trusting me, baby.” I had not realized that I had tears rolling down my face. “Hey,” he says as he wipes my tears. “Are those tears of joy or sadness?” Concern is etched on his face.

“Complete and utter joy,” I say as I kiss his nose. “I love you, Kyren. Thank you for healing my heart and soul.”

I hear him whisper, “My pleasure, Ms. Milby.”

I drift off into a deep and restful sleep.

Chapter 16

The week passes quickly. Kyren has been busy putting finishing touches on this client's yacht. I worked longer days than normal, so we have only been able to talk or send text through the phone.

Kyren acted very shy on Saturday after we made love. I think he was just very unsure of himself. I reassured him by returning the favor by slowly and gently making love to him that day. After that, he was a happy man. And then it ended up to just downright dirty fucking in his truck before he left. I have decided with Kyren, I like it both ways, the kinky fucking and the vanilla.

Kyren has made arrangements for Mrs. Moore to cater a dinner at my house tonight for Zade and Cady's homecoming. He is bringing his uncle Tom. Even though we have only spoken a few times, I really like him.

Cady and Zade are arriving at the airport at the same time, but they refused to let me pick them up. I didn't realize that Kyren secretly made plans to get them himself.

I hear a knock at the door, already knowing it's Kyren. I don't understand why he always knocks. After all, he let Uncle Tom in without my permission. You would think he would be comfortable just walking in without knocking.

I open the door to a squeal. It's Cady, Zade, Kyren, and Uncle Tom all at once. Before I can say a word, Cady has me in a bear hug.

"I have missed you so much," she shouts against my ear. We are giggling like teenage girls. When she finally lets go, I get my first look at Zade. He looks great, strong, and healthy. It's the first time I have seen him not gaunt and pale. He simply looks beautiful. I find myself running into his arms.

"Zade, you look so good."

He breaks free of my hold and runs his hands down my arms, patting me in a way as if to make sure that I am real. "You look good too, kiddo."

"Kiddo? I haven't heard that in years." Oh, how I have missed it. I pull back and glare at Kyren. "You are one sneaky man," I say, pointing my finger at him.

"Hey, just trying to make my baby utterly happy." His hands are raised in surrender.

"You are forgiven," I say with a wide smile.

"Then how about one of those hugs?" I willingly go into his arms, and we kiss. Then the kiss turns passionate. We have forgotten we are not alone. When we release one another, all eyes are on us, and their mouths are gaping open. I shrug and smile and walk away as Kyren slaps my ass. All of them burst into laughter, including Uncle Tom.

Mrs. Moore has completely outdone herself. There is enough food for an army. Of course, the way Kyren and Zade eat, they are an army all on their own. I sit back and enjoy the conversations going on at the dinner table. I'm half listening to Cady rattle on about her and Jon. Kyren, Zade, and Uncle Tom are all very comfortable with one another. It's like they have been friends all their lives. This is it. This is what Zade and I have missed our entire lives—family. A normal family. God, this feels so good.

"Earth to Brogan," I hear loudly. I look over at Cady.

"Just what?" Zade encourages.

"I was just thinking how wonderful it feels to finally have a family." Tears mist my eyes.

After dinner, Cady disappears into her room. Probably for her nightly call to Jon, or it could be just to give me some time with Zade. Mrs. Moore has packed up and is headed back to the yacht.

"Thank you so much, Mrs. Moore, for all of your hard work. I wish you would have let me help you."

"Don't be silly, dear. I love doing this. Besides, I get paid very well to cater for Mr. Nolan."

"Here, I will help you load this stuff in the truck," Uncle Tom says.

"Are you guys leaving?" I ask as Kyren steps up.

"We are leaving, baby. Zade is staying for tonight so you can catch up after that he has agreed to stay with me on the yacht."

"Don't be silly. He can stay here in my room. I will sleep on the couch."

Zade chimes in, "No offense, kiddo, but I've heard all about Kyren's yacht, and I would rather stay on a manly yacht than a girly cottage."

"Traitor," I say, laughing at Zade. "And you, mister," I say, playfully slapping Kyren's chest, "I've lost you to another man," as I cover my wounded heart.

"Not likely, baby. I can't keep up with you. Why would I every need anyone else?"

"And don't you forget it, mister."

"Believe me. I'm sure you won't let me."

I lean closer to him, "Speaking of which, it's been awhile, the phone sexting is great, but I'd like to get my hands on the real thing."

"A little hard right now."

I step in even closer and rub my hand between us, over his crotch. "It doesn't feel hard to me."

He growls in my ear, and the next thing I know, I am upside down and hanging from Kyren's shoulder. I squeal. "If you, gentlemen, would excuse us a minute, I have to teach Ms. Milby a lesson or two."

They all laugh and part to let Kyren pass. I am laughing and red faced at the same time. I smack his ass. """You wouldn't dare." I laugh.

"Oh, baby, I do believe you just dared me," he says as I see my bedroom door shut. He carries me straight into the shower.

"Seriously, Kyren, put me down now," I yell at him.

"I intend to, but I need the shower running to drown out the noise."

"Noise? What noise?"

"The sound of me fucking you."

Chapter 17

Kyren walks out the front door to the guys leaning against the truck.

"Lesson over?" Zade says smirking.

"Yep."

"Must have taken her awhile to learn her lesson," Zade says, laughing.

"Well, she is a hardheaded, demanding woman," Kyren says as he slams his truck door. Uncle Tom, Zade, and Mrs. Moore break into laughter.

"I like him," Zade states as he walks back the door. "He's perfect for you, kiddo. He doesn't take your shit."

"Better yet," I add, "he doesn't care about all my broken shit. He has healed my heart, and I trust him completely."

"I can see that. I'm glad you found him."

"He actually found me, and then he saved me. Zade, Dr. Kohl says you're really good. Is it true?"

"I am, Brogan. I'm stronger than ever." He wraps me in his arms.

I hold him tight. "You look good. I've never seen you with any meat on your bones."

He squeezes me. "Back at you, kiddo."

Now I think he is holding me tight as a defensive move. "Are you calling me fat, Zade?"

"No." He pauses, then continues, "Not at all, but the starving look wasn't working for you."

I lean back to look at him, and for a brief moment, I see sadness. "No, I guess it didn't for either of us."

"Brogan, I feel free of the past at last."

"I can honestly say, me too." We hug again.

"Hey, sis, do you have any cards?"

Whoa quick change of subject, but I know exactly what he is thinking. "Slapjack?" I can't help but grin. It was our one good memory as kids.

He lets go. "I'll grab some beer. You go find the cards."

Cady comes out of her room as we are setting up. "What are you guys up to?"

"Slapjack. Want to join us?"

"I play winner," she says, grinning. "I love that game."

The three of us play, laugh, drink, and tell stories until two in the morning. Zade insists on the couch. I crawl into bed with a sense of peace and happiness. The only thing missing is Kyren. I fall asleep thinking of him.

I wake the next morning, way too early, to my phone ringing. "What!" I snap.

"Well, good morning, sunshine. I assume you haven't had your coffee yet."

"My eyes aren't even open yet, Kyren!"

"Late night?" He is laughing

"What time is it?"

"Noon."

"Shit!" Half the damn day is gone.

"I figured you guys would be up late. I am at your front door with loads of your favorite coffee."

"God, I love you. Get your gorgeous ass in here."

I hear the front door open, and before I can even get out of bed, he is in the doorway.

"Hey, beautiful." His gaze is all over my body.

"Argg! Just get over here and pour the coffee in my mouth." He laughs.

"Come on, baby. Get out of bed before I come over there and strip you naked."

Now that's an incentive for me to stay right where I am, so I pull the covers off and seductively lay back down. He walks over to the bed, and I think for a moment from his hungry look that he is going to join me, but instead, he inhales and hands me a coffee. I take it, feeling disappointed.

"As much as I would love to join you, I believe you have forgotten about our fishing trip today." He is smirking at me.

I breathe in the coffee. Damn, I did forget. I take a sip and get out of bed.

"Good girl. Zade and Cady have already gone out for breakfast, and they are waiting at my place."

I stand on my tippy toes and kiss his lips quickly. "Give me two minutes." I scurry off to the bathroom, brush my teeth and hair, and head to the closet. I put on a skimpy teal-colored bikini, cover-up, and flip-flops. I go back into the bedroom where Kyren remains. "Okay, I'm ready."

"You sure clean up fast," he says as he peeks under my cover-up. "Damn, girl! How's a man supposed to fish with a hard on?"

"Well, we could put some bait on it and use it as a fishing pole."

"Ouch! Okay, that will get rid of it for now, but don't shake that gorgeous ass in my face all day." He slaps my ass as he says it.

"I absolutely will," I say as I grab him for a heated kiss.

"You are going to be the death of me, woman," he says through clenched teeth.

"Oh, but what a way to go," I say as we head out the door.

He smacks my ass again as I climb into his truck in my usual unladylike fashion.

"Hey, my client is back in town, and he said he could meet up with us tomorrow."

"Okay. My last demon to slay," I say, half joking.

He looks at me and laughs. "Okay, demon slayer, I will call you with a meeting time tomorrow."

"By the way, what is my demons name?"

"Bob Miller."

I grin at him. "Tomorrow consider Bob Miller slayed."

"You ain't right, girl," he says as he drags me to sit next to him in the truck.

We fish all day. We are sunburnt, and we have all had way too much beer to drink. We dock at a local dive on the water. We are all famished.

"Oh my god! They have the best fish tacos," I say around a mouthful of food.

"Yea, and the view isn't bad either." Zade's eyes are following a girl to the bar. I smack his arm. "What? I am a healthy male with needs."

"Gross. I have never seen that side of you."

"Well, I have never seen my sister thrown over a he man's shoulder before and drag off to her bedroom and—"

"Okay, okay, okay! I get your point." My face feels red, and not from the sunburn. "Go get her then, tiger." Shooing him away with my hands.

"If you guys will excuse me, I want to check in with Jon," Cady says as she walks away.

"Alone at last." Kyren slides closer. I feel his hand slip up my thigh.

"Missed me much," I say through pouted lips.

"I have been dying to peel you out of that damn bikini." He nips my ear.

"Damn, you have gone and done it again." I bite at his chin.

"What?"

"I'm wet."

"Good. I have suffered the entire day with a hard on. The least you can do is be ready and wet." His hand slips higher.

"Bathroom. Out back. Now!" I'm out of my chair. It is a single bathroom and no one is around. As soon as I step in, Kyren is shoving me through the door and locking it.

He wastes no time. "Bend over the sink," he commands hoarsely. I bend to take off my bikini, and he stops me. "Just bend over."

"But I thought you wanted to peel me out of it."

"I will work around them," as he pushes my bottoms to the side and slams into me.

"Fuck!" I scream.

He stills. "I'm sorry, baby. I needed in you so badly. Did I hurt you?"

"No, I want more." And that is all it takes. He slams me into the sink. I have to brace myself.

"Baby, I can't stop. Reach in between us and touch yourself." I immediately obey. I find that little nub and begin rubbing circles. He is pumping in and out so hard, it doesn't take either one of us long before we both explode. As we both find our release, I hear a knock on the door, and if that isn't bad enough, I hear the familiar voice of Cady. Kyren starts laughing.

I whisper, "It's not funny, Kyren. Cady is all vanilla. She will be so embarrassed."

"Clean up. She will survive."

"Whoever is in there needs to hurry up. I really have to pee!"

Kyren opens the door with a shit-eating grin.

"Oh my god! You two are awful! You, mister, need to keep it in your pants, and you"—she is pointing at me, red faced and glaring at me—"well…well…I'm just happy for you. Now get out! I really have to pee! Please just tell me you didn't do it on the toilet."

"Sink," Kyren says quickly, and I smack his arm.

"Gah! You two are just too kinky," she says as she slams the door.

"Kyren, you were no help at all."

"That's not what you said a few minutes ago."

I grab his hand to leave. "Bastard. Come on. Let's find Zade."

Zade is at the bar, all cozied up to some blonde. "Hey, Zade, I'm ready to go. It's been a long day. I'm sunburnt and dirty and in need of a shower.

"You are a dirty girl, and I like it." I hear as I feel a nip at my ear. I yelp.

"Kyren, behave. Haven't you caused enough embarrassment today?"

"It's so hard, literally."

I turn to whisper in his ear, "I thought we just took care of that?"

"Oh, baby, I am so not done with you."

I swallow hard and turn back around to Zade laughing at me like he knew what. He whispered, "You two are obviously in need of some alone time bad. Cady and I will hangout for a while. I'm sure we can find a way home." He winks at the blonde, who is hanging all over him.

"Okay, you stay, but we will take Cady home. I'm sure she would rather listen to us have hot sex than watch you pick up a stranger."

"Um, that was not a mental picture I needed in my head about my sister," Zade says, scrunching his face at me. "But you go have fun while I work my own magic." He is all smiles. "Love you, sis," he adds and blows me a kiss.

"Love you too." I think to myself how easy that was to say to him. I smile to myself and hug him.

Kyren grabs my hand. "Let's go find Cady."

On the way home, Cady talks our ears off. I am having a hard time keeping up because my mind is on Kyren's words, "I'm not done with you yet." I am as bad as he is. I can't wait to get home to have my way with him.

Cady is still talking as we walk through the front door, but all I focus on is the heat in Kyren's eyes. It's definitely desire.

"Um, Cady sweetie, can we finish this conversation later? I would really like a shower and turn in early."

Before she has even responded, I hear the shower turn on. "You two can't keep your hands off each other," she says with her hands on her hips.

"Well, look at him, Cady. He's got a hot body, abs to die for, and his—"

"STOP! I don't want to hear about his cock!"

I burst out laughing. I have never heard Cady use the C word before. "I was going to say his ass is very bitable, but he does have a beautiful cock."

"Oh gah! Brogan, just go get in the shower." She's laughing now too.

I walk to my bedroom door and turn to Cady. "Cady?"

"What more do you want to torture me with?"

"I love you." I hear Kyren call my name.

"Oh, I love you too. Now go take care of Kyren before he does it himself." She laughs and walks away.

I enter the bathroom. Kyren is stark naked, but not in the shower. He turns and I see his beautiful thick hard cock in his hand. "Why didn't you get in?" I'm licking my lips.

"I told you I wanted to strip you out of that bikini." He eagerly pulls at my straps, and my top falls to the floor. I see him pumping himself roughly.

"Would you like some help with that handful?" I am now biting my lip.

"No, because the minute your hands are on me, *it* will be *over*." He lets go and grabs both of my wrists and pulls them behind my back. He takes my bikini top and binds my elbows. I am so glad he didn't tie my wrists. I don't know how I would have reacted. I am bound by my own swimsuit; it makes my breasts stick out, and Kyren is already enjoying them. He is sucking and pinching them really hard.

"Kyren." I am already begging.

"Oh, baby, there is no need to beg. You will get exactly what you want and need, but you are being punished first."

"What? Punished? For what?" I ask, a little too excited.

"You wiggling that fine ass in front of me all day. You rubbed it against me every chance you got."

"You noticed," I say, gasping for air because he is being relentless on my nipples.

"Baby, I notice everything you do. Every lick of your lips, every sexual noise you make when you're within ten feet of me."

Arggg! I feel that pull way down. He suddenly stops. "No don't stop," I rasp.

"I'm not letting you come yet, and I can tell you are close."

"No no no. Not close at all," I groan and bite my lip.

"That little lie, baby, just added two more swats to that sweet ass of yours."

I gulp. I am so fucking wet and excited. I love this man and I love what he does to me. I love the rough kinky side of him and I even have come to love his soft passionate side. Kyren sits on the tub and maneuvers me over his lap, my ass firmly in the air.

"I love your ass, I love the way it turns pink when I smack it." Then I feel a hard firm smack on the lower part of my ass where my thighs meet. I moan with pleasure. He rubs the area then smacks me again. "Count baby, twelve smacks for your naughty behavior and little lie."

"Two." *Smack*. "Three." *Smack*. "Four…"

By the time he gets to twelve, I am ready to burst. He rubs my ass and then sends me to my knees between his thighs. I lick my lips at the sight of his now even thicker cock. I glance up at him. "Untie me."

"Not yet. I just want your mouth on me."

I need no other prodding. I suck in just the tip of his cock ,and I hear him groan.

"Fuck!"

The sound of him turned on is all I need. I slide all the way down his cock, sucking and licking as I go. His hands are on my shoulders, roughly pushing me down. I unsheathe my teeth and pull upward. I hear an animalistic growl and feel him pull my hair.

"Enough!" he yells. "I don't want to come in your mouth. I want to be inside of you." He is kissing me hard and untying me at the same time. "Up, baby. In the shower."

Before I even move, he pulls off my bikini bottoms, picks me up, and I wrap my legs around him. He steps in the shower, and we are under the spray of the water. I'm gasping for air from his assault on my mouth and the water flowing over me.

"Kyren, please now." I sound so desperate. He leans me against the cool tile and grabs his cock and plunges deep inside me. I explode immediately. I can't control it. I am literally shaking from my orgasm. It's so intense. Kyren has stilled. When I stop shaking, he pulls out of me. I slide down his body, and he turns me around. He bends me how he wants me, and then I feel his hand circling my anal opening. My eyes fly open. He instinctively rubs my back.

"It's okay, baby. I won't hurt you." I feel stick a finger inside me there. I squirm. Then with his other hand, he puts the tip of his cock inside me. "Relax, baby. I promise you will come quickly. This time I'm coming with you." Kyren slowly pushes all the way in. I feel so full with his cock fully inside me. Then he begins to really move.

"Holy fuck," I scream and explode around him again and, this time, taking him with me. As I come down from my orgasm, I slide to the floor of the tub. I faintly hear Kyren whispering something to me, but I can't make out the word. I am exhausted.

"Brogan? Are you okay?"

"Hmmmmm…"

"Baby, are you coherent?"

"Hmmmmm."

"Can you just tell me if I hurt you? Was it too much?" He sounds a little frightened. That awakens me a little.

"Kyren, it was perfect," was all I could manage to say. Then I feel him lifting me to my feet. He washes me, and I wince when he gets to my ass.

"I'd say I'm sorry, baby, but I rather enjoyed it."

"Me too." I cuddle on his chest. He finishes washing me then quickly washes himself. He grabs two towels—one, he dries and wraps my hair in; the other, he uses to dry my body. He grabs another towel and hurriedly dries his beautiful body. He lifts me and carries me to bed. He pulls back the sheets and removes my towels. He lays me down.

"Sleep, baby," he whispers as he kisses the top of my head. I feel the sheets cover me, but I don't feel the familiar dip of the bed as he crawls in. I hear him dressing.

"Kyren, you aren't staying?" I barely get out through my sleepy haze.

"No, baby. I have an early meeting in town. I will call you in the morning." I pout. "No pouting, or I will have to spank you again."

"As good as that sounds, I am just too exhausted," I say dreamily. "Kyren?"

"Yeah, baby?"

"Love you."

He leans in and kisses my nose. "I love you too, baby." I don't even hear him leave. I fall fast asleep.

Chapter 18

I wake to Cady jumping on my bed. “Wake up! I need some girl time.”

“Cady, it’s seven in the morning,” I say, and I draw the sheets over my head.

“Please, Brogan.” Now she is full out whining. “As soon as your day starts, you will be off with the boys,” and now she’s pouting.

True. My thoughts turn to Kyren, and I smile. “Okay, Cady.” I start to sit up but realize I’m naked about the same time Cady does. She hops up, grabs a shirt from my dresser, and throws it at me and proceeds to find me some panties.

“Your sex life is great isn’t it?”

“Um, yeah. Where is this coming from Cady you never want to talk about sex?”

“Well, it’s just that sometimes I think Jon and I are not really as exciting as you and Kyren.” She is knotting her fingers together, and her face is bright red.

“Oh, Cady, is something wrong between you and Jon?”

“No, it’s just, well…we always have sex in bed, not in some restaurant bathroom or truck or a shower.”

My mouth falls open. “Really? Never?”

She bites her lip and looks up. “Never.”

“Have you talked to Jon about it?”

"No. We don't talk about sex. You know that old saying that was beat into my head, good girls don't talk about sex."

"Cady, you have to tell him what you want and need. Talking to someone you love about sex isn't dirty. You might find out he wants to change things up a bit too."

She pauses for a minute. "But what if he doesn't?"

"Jon loves you. He wants you. Seduce him, Cady. Get some sexy lingerie and, better yet, just be naked when he walks in the door."

"Brogan, you are a lot braver than I am."

I reach over and dig through my nightstand. "I have a book for you." I hand it to her, and her face appears even redder. "I have lots of highlights." I flip through a few pages to show her. "This one is sure to spice things up."

Cady stops to read the highlighted words. "Holy shit, Brogan!" she says laughing.

"Have fun, sweetie, and enjoy him. Don't think of any part of sex as being dirty or wrong. As long as both partners are consenting, there is nothing wrong with it. And the dirtier, the better."

She points at the highlighted page. "You think Jon would consent to this?" The picture on the page is of a woman tied to a St. Andrew's cross.

"With you, yes." We both laugh.

"Thanks, Brogan. I feel better." She leans in and grabs me for a bear hug. Something, not too long ago, we would have never done. Cady starts to leave the room and turns. "He's good for you."

I don’t need to ask who. “He has made me whole.” As the words leave my mouth, my cell phone rings, and I can’t help but smile.

“Good morning, Kyren.”

He must have guessed I was smiling from my voice. “Hey, baby. You’re up early and in a good mood.”

“Well, when a girl is completely satiated by the man that she is madly in love with, it’s easy to be happy.”

“Completely satiated, aye?” He has a low, sexy growl to his voice.

“Completely,” is my only response.

“Well, I have to figure out a way to insatiate you so I can satiate you all over again.”

I love teasing Kyren. “Feel free to satiate me anytime and anywhere you like, baby.”

This time he literally growls into the phone. “Now that I have a raging hard on, I have to go into a meeting. I just called to tell you to meet Bob at one o’clock in his yacht.”

“Oh, I had forgotten about slaying the beast today.”

“You will be fine.” His voice is much softer now.

“I’d rather slay that hard on you are sporting.”

“Jesus, Brogan. I swear you are going to kill me.”

“Love you, baby. Go to your meeting.” I can’t help but giggle at him.

“Go slay your dragon, and I’ll call you later.” He hangs up the phone.

I slip out of bed and find some shorts and head for the kitchen for massive amounts of coffee. I start calling for Zade because he is not on the couch. He doesn't answer.

"Um, he must not have come home last night," Cady says as she pours me some coffee.

"Way to go, Zade," I say with a fist pump in the air.

"Ick, Brogan. A one-night stand?" Cady's face matches her tone.

"Cady, we all have needs, even my brother."

"I'm just saying I think Zade deserves better don't you think?"

I stop and put my coffee on the counter and turn to her. "Cady, are you jealous that Zade was with a woman?"

"What! Uh, no! He's like my brother," she says, but not convincingly.

"Cady, are you sure you and Jon are okay?" Now I am a little concerned. I reach out and hold her hand, which is totally out of character for me.

For a brief moment, I see unshed tears in Cady's eyes. She hesitates a little too long. I squeeze her hand, so she will look directly at me. "We are fine, Brogan. We are just in a lull." A single tear falls down her cheek.

"Is there anything I can do to help?"

"I think your book may be enough," she whispers.

I know that Cady had a thing for Zade when we were in college, but she never acted on it because of me. I just wonder if being around him has brought up some old, unmet desire for him. They were friendly in the boat yesterday. I thought they were just catching up, but maybe I was being naïve, or maybe, Cady is just trying hard to not have feelings for him. I finally release her hand.

"Okay, Cady, but I'm here if you need me. You can tell me anything. No matter what, you are my best friend. There are no judgements here." Cady has always struggled to do the right thing in everyone's eyes. I just want her to be happy and follow her heart.

She finally turns away, and I see her swipe her cheek. "Drink your coffee, Brogan, and quit worrying about me. Zade called, and I am going to pick him up at his floozy's house."

There is that hint of jealousy again. But this time, I ignore it. "Okay. I need to get dressed anyways. I have a meeting at one."

"I'm out of here," Cady says as she heads for the door.

"Cady?" She turns my direction. "Zade and I are good now."

"And?" She looks puzzled.

"And nothing. Just tell Zade I'll see him later."

Cady opens her mouth to say something, but instead, she turns and leaves.

After an entire pot of coffee, I decide it's time to get dressed. I want to wear something sexy for Kyren, yet I have the meeting first with Bob Miller, which I am tempted to blow off. But Kyren set up the meeting, so I feel obligated.

I decide on a white pair of shorts with a blue-stripped sailor top that's off one shoulder and a cute pair of navy stripped slip-ons. Comfortable yet a little sexy, at least what I think is sexy. I apply light makeup and wear my hair down. I have a plan in mind for

Kyren. I think we should live together. This is a big step for me. I've never thought of living with a man before him. I just want to wake up with him every morning. When did I become so mushy? I hate to give up my place, but I know how much Kyren loves his yacht, and I love Kyren. I've already changed so much for him. Living with him would be an easy one. I just don't know how he feels about it, but I intend to find out.

I take my boat as usual. I'm excited to see the finished yacht the Kyren built for Bob Miller. I arrive about ten minutes early and don't see Bob, but I decide to let myself in. He's not living on it yet, so I know that I won't be interrupting anything.

I walk in, and I am amazed by the craftsmanship of the woodwork. The inside reminds me of a cabin you would find in the mountains. It is simply beautiful, but it gives me an eerie feeling of a home long forgotten.

I make my way down to the bottom floor with a feeling of unease but a desire to explore. I find the master suite, and I still at the scent in the air. I am immediately taken back ten years. I'm hyperventilating and nauseated. I need to meet my fears head on. I tell myself to breathe, just breathe, attempting to slow my breaths. From behind me, I hear footsteps. I turn to meet the voice of the man calling my name, and my nightmares become real.

Chapter 19

It's him. It's not possible, but it's him. I see the pure evil in his eyes. He looks as surprised and horrified as I am.

"You're not Bob Miller." It comes out as a whisper and a gasp.

"And you're not Brogan." He stares straight through me

"But how are you alive? I saw you die." I am trembling.

"You saw me fall and left me for dead, but I most certainly did not die that day." He takes a step toward me.

I instinctively take a step back. "But I shot you."

"Correction, you and that smartass brother of yours shot me!"

"Leave Zade out of this." I am screaming at him.

"Trust me, kitten. I am happy to deal with just you." He takes another step closer.

I feel sick. The name kitten makes me want to hurl. "Don't ever call me kitten! I'm not the same little weak girl you terrorized. You touch me, and I will kill you all over again!"

"Oh, kitten," he purrs. "You have spunk now, I will love the challenge."

I look around for anything I can use as a weapon, but the room is empty. He steps toward me again, and I step backward.

"Kitten, just make this easy and be still."

I decide my only out is to let him close enough to kick his ass. He reaches for me, and I reach out and grab his arm and twist it behind him. He yelps. I put him on the ground with my knee between his shoulder blade, and I start screaming at him.

"Ray Milby, you will never touch me or Zade again!" I am yelling between gritted teeth. I twist his arm again, and he yells.

"How did you come up with the name Brogan?" he yells out.

"It was the closes to broken I could come up with. You did that. You broke me, but never again!" I say as I apply more pressure between his shoulder blades. "Kailey Milby is long gone, and I am not broken or weak any longer." I apply even more pressure. "I could easily break your spine, but that would be an easy way out for you."

I fish my cell phone out of my pocket. But instead of calling 911, I dial Kyren, but before he can answer, my father flips over, and when he does, he pulls out a gun from the front of his pants. I immediately turn and head for the door to escape him.

I hear the gunfire. I fall but don't feel any pain. My mind is racing. Did I fall out of fear or did I get shot? I attempt to get up, but find my answer as I fall back down. Now there is pain. My right leg is bleeding. There is blood everywhere. Oh my god! He really shot me. I apply pressure to my leg.

Now he is standing over me with the gun pointed at my head. I frantically try to get up again, but blood starts spewing from my leg. Ray bends down. As he does, he is removing his belt. He hands it to me and tells me to strap it around my leg.

I hesitate. I could grab it and strike him with it in hopes that he drops the gun, but if I bleed out, he wins.

"Don't even think about it," he says as he presses the gun to my temple.

I strap the belt to the top of my thigh and pull it just enough to stop the bleeding. Ray is now standing above me. He reaches behind him and sticks the gun in the back of his pants. Then he grabs me by the hair with both hands and starts dragging me back in the room.

I scream out in pain. "Stop, please Ray. Don't do this!"

He ignores me, and he is pulling me in the closet. I see my cell phone on the floor. I can see Kyren's name lit up. I can only hope we were connected. I scream out again in hopes that Kyren will hear me.

"Please, Ray! Don't lock me in the closet. Please let me go!"

"Oh, kitten, I have plans for you, and none of them involves letting you go. I know that stupid brother of yours must be here too."

My protective instincts come out. "Leave Zade alone! I haven't seen him in years because of you!" I start kicking him with my left leg. He pulls out the gun again, and I stilled.

"Zade will come, kitten." He leans over and grabs my phone. He pushes end and starts searching for his number. He smiles and shows me the face of the phone that now displays Zade's number.

"Please, Ray, I will do whatever you want. I won't fight you, just ,please, leave Zade alone." I am pleading with him, and tears are rolling down my face. The thought of ever letting him touch me is abhorrent, but I won't let him near Zade.

"Is that so?" he purrs. "Get up then."

I struggle to my feet. "On the shelf above you is a rope. Grab it," he demands as he points the gun at me. I struggle to get it, ignoring the pain in my leg. He moves closer, and then with his free hand, he starts winding the rope around my wrists like he did so many years ago. He then lifts my arms and ties them to a metal hoop at the top of the closet, obviously custom built for whatever he had planned.

He steps back and smiles. “That’s better, kitten.” He then hits the call button on my phone.

I scream at him. “You son of a bitch! I did what you wanted, now leave him the fuck alone.” I am pulling desperately, trying to free the rope.

“Well hello, son of mine. What’s the matter? Don’t you believe in ghosts?” He listens for a moment. “I can prove it. Say hello, kitten.”

I say nothing. Maybe Zade won’t believe him. “Speak, kitten!” he demands as he puts the gun to my face. I still say nothing, and he hits me with the butt of the gun, and everything goes dark.

Chapter 20

Oh fuck! My head hurts. Something is running down my face. I go to rub it and realize I am still bound. It all comes flooding back, and nausea overwhelms me. It's dark in here. The closet door is shut, and I hear yelling. I recognize the voices. It's Kyren and Ray.

Suddenly the door flies open: Kyren and Ray are pointing guns at each other. "I told you to put your goddamn gun down!" Ray is screaming at Kyren. He turns and puts the gun in my face. "Kyren, please no," I beg him.

"I'm not leaving you to this asshole. You want someone, you coward? Take me and let her go!" Kyren's hands are in the air.

"Put your gun down and kick it over here," Ray says, laughing.

Kyren complies.

"Okay, hero. I will kill one of you. Which one shall it be?" Ray is waving his gun back and forth at us.

"Me!" we both scream at the same time.

"How romantic. Both of you so willing to die for the other."

My mind is racing. Kyren has to be frantic. He has to be flashing back to Joe. I won't allow him to choose. I am pulling at my ropes and screaming at Kyren to get out of here.

Kyren is talking in a low tone to Ray. While Ray is distracted, I pull hard on my ropes, and it gives. And just as it does, Zade and Cady burst through the doors. All hell breaks loose, and there is gunfire. I see Cady fall to the ground. Kyren is struggling with Ray. I grab the gun that Kyren had put down. Zade is at my side.

Zade reaches for the gun. "No, Zade, don't touch the gun. Please, go get Cady out of here," I plead. It takes all my strength to get up. I aim the gun at Ray, but Kyren is too close to him.

I yell out, "Kyren, move!" And I keep the gun pointed in Ray's direction.

Kyren gives Ray one more punch to the head, then in one swift move, he reaches and grabs the gun from my hand and puts two bullets in Ray's head.

Ray is limp on the floor. Kyren reaches down to feel for a pulse, but I know there is none. He stands straight up and turns to look at me. "He is dead for real this time," is all that he says.

I exhale, not realizing I had been holding my breath. Zade rushes back in the room. His eyes skim over to the body on the floor and then back at me.

"Is he…"

"Yes," I whisper. "Zade, where is Cady?"

"I carried her to the deck and called 911. I heard a gunshot, and I came back to see…" He can't get the words out as he squeezes his eyes shut and runs his hands through his hair.

"Zade, look at me!"

He looks up at me.

"I'm alive. I need to know how Cady is."

"Not good, Brogan. Kyren's uncle is with her."

I hear sirens. “Please take me to her,” I rasp out before I collapse to the floor.

Kyren reaches me first and picks me up and carries me to the deck where there are now swarms of police and ambulances. I’m barely conscious, but I hear familiar medical jargon being thrown around.

“We are losing her. Give another round of epi. Continue CPR.”

I am no longer strong enough to speak, and I can only see through the slits in my eyelids. Kyren places me on a gurney, and I hear Zade talking to the paramedics. Kyren walks a few feet away and is surrounded by police. I finally give into the darkness.

Chapter 21

I wake to the sound of alarms. I have IVs and lines hooked to me. I slowly open my eyes, and I see Zade slumped over in a chair, asleep. Kyren is sitting, bent over, with his head on the bed. I reach over and touch Kyren's hair. He jumps straight up, startling me and waking Zade.

"Hey, baby," I whisper as I look into his beautiful bruised face. He says nothing; he just stares at me. Zade is all over me hugging me.

"Oh god, Brogan! You're okay. You are really okay." I wince in pain, and he lets go. "I'm so sorry, sis."

Kyren is still silent. "My leg?" I reach down to make sure it is still there.

Kyren finally breaks his silence. "You lost a lot of blood. You were in surgery for hours. The doctor says, in time, you will make a full recovery." As he speaks, his face shows no emotion. He is scaring me. I reach to touch his hand, and he allows it, but he leans back into his chair, further out of reach. I can't feel or see any emotion from his eyes. They are hollow.

I suddenly remember Cady being shot. I turn to look at Zade, who is hovering over me. "Cady?"

Tears instantly fill Zade's eyes. I gasp.

"She's in a coma," Kyren states flatly.

"Oh my god! Is she…" My eyes now flowing with tears.

Zade takes my hand. "It's been two days since…since the accident. She's on a vent, but there has been no…"—he swallows—"no response."

I'm now in a full-blown cry as Zade cradles me, and I feel Kyren release my hand. "Two days? Where is Jon?" I manage between sobs.

"Jon is with her. He hasn't left her side." Kyren is now up and pacing the room.

Before Zade releases me, I whisper in his ear, "I love you, but can I have a minute with Kyren?" He hugs me again quickly and lightly kisses my cheek.

He covers for me. "I need to go give Jon a break and get an update on Cady."

Kyren is standing at the end of the bed and staring at me. "I'm so sorry," I say between sobs. "I never meant for you to get hurt. All these years, I thought Ray was dead." Tears are running down his face, but he remains just staring at me. "Please, please say something to me," I beg him.

I see him inhale. "I murdered another man, Brogan."

"No, Kyren, you didn't murder Joe, and you saved me from that monster. That's not murder." I am frantically trying to get out of bed. I rip off my telemetry and yank out my IV. My leg is in a cast, and I'm still weak. I just so want to hold him, but I am unable to get out of bed. Kyren slowly moves to the side of the bed and sits back down. Blood is dripping down my arm where I pulled out my IV. A nurse comes running through the door.

"Ms. Milby, you need to lie back down," she says as she tends to my arm.

"I'm fine. Please just leave us alone."

Kyren stands. "No, Brogan, she is right. You need to lie back down." I lie back down, but our eyes are locked. He looks beaten, like he wants to flee. God, I can't lose him now. I've got to reach him somehow. I need to touch him. I need him to touch me.

The nurse has reattached everything but my IV. "I will give you a few minutes, but I will be back to replace your IV. You need the fluids." She walks out.

"Kyren, what is it?" I whisper. He looks away. "Look at me."

He inhales deeply and turns his eyes to mine, and all I see is ice-cold eyes. I literally shiver. "Kyren…*I love you.*"

"I know, baby," he says, but there is no softness in his voice. "But I … I can't do…us."

Tears well up again. I tell myself to breathe. "Why, Kyren?" I barely get the words out. He comes and sits on the side of the bed with me. He doesn't touch me, so I lean up and wrap my arms around his shoulders. "Kyren, what you did was heroic. You are an amazingly strong man. You *are* a *good* man." I say each word firmly and slowly. He remains quiet, but I see a single tear roll down his cheek. With my lips, I wipe it away. He suddenly jumps up. His back is to me. His head falls forward, and his shoulders slump.

"Kyren." He turns and stares at me. "Kyren." It's a plea.

"Brogan…I am broken." I inhale sharply because I know that pain. My tears continue to fall. "I can't do this. I'm no good for you."

A sob escapes me. "Kyren, that's just not true. You are the best thing that has ever happened to me. You are the best part of me. You saved me from myself, and then you saved my life. Kyren, please don't do this. Don't do this to yourself, and don't do this to us." I am frantic now because I see no light in his eyes. They are so empty.

"God knows I love you, Brogan." Oh thank God! He is at least talking. "But I'm done."

"No, Kyren, no." I squeeze my eyes shut and shake my head. I only thought I knew pain before, but my heart is breaking.

He leans down and kisses my forehead. "Good-bye, baby," he whispers hoarsely. He walks toward the door. I rip everything off again and try to get out of bed so that I can stop him from leaving. The door flies open, and the nurse rushes in the door. She moves in front of me, blocking my path to Kyren. I lean around her to see Kyren, but he is already gone.

"NO!" I scream and try to push pass the nurse. Before I know it, there are multiple white coats surrounding me, then I feel the sharp jab of the needle in my thigh. I know in that instant there is no way of fighting. I fall back onto the bed and wait for the darkness to take over.

Chapter 22

I open my eyes, and oh, thank God it was a nightmare. I was dreaming. I can see a blurry face in front of me. “Kyren?”

“No, sis, it’s Zade.” He sounds sad.

“Where is he?” Please, God, let have been a dream. I feel him touch my hand.

“He’s gone.” I can almost hear the pity in his voice.

I sit straight up and feel pain shoot through my leg. “What do you mean gone, Zade?”

“He came by Cady’s room.” He hesitates. “He broke down, Brogan. He loves you, but he is tormented by his demons.”

I start screaming at Zade, “Why didn’t you make him stay, Zade!” Tears are freely flowing from my eyes.

“I tried, Brogan. I tried to get him to Dr. Kohl, but he refused.” I hear and see the pain in Zade’s face.

“Zade, help me up, help me get out of here. I need to see Cady and then find him.”

“Brogan, your leg was severely injured, and you are still weak from the blood loss.”

“I don’t give a fuck about my leg, Zade. Help me up!”

He moves to the side of the bed and puts his arms around my waist and lifts me to my feet. A wave of nausea comes over me from the pain. “Give me a second,” I say as I concentrate on breathing. In through the nose, out through the mouth.

“Oh, fuck it!” Zade reaches down and cradles me in his arms.

Two nurses run into the room. “She needs to be in bed.” They are pulling at Zade’s arms.

Zade starts yelling back at them. “She needs to see her friend. Either help me or get the fuck out of my way!”

“All right,” one of the nurses concedes, “but let me get a wheelchair so that neither of you get injured.” Her tone is very firm. The other nurse has disappeared, and Zade stands firm with me in his arms. The other nurse comes back, pushing a wheelchair, and Zade gently places me in it.

“I will take care of her. You can follow if you want,” he says in a little softer tone.

He takes me to Cady’s side. Jon is asleep in a chair at her bedside. I whisper, not wanting to wake him. “Cady.” I squeeze her hand. Her head is wrapped in gauze, and her eyes are swollen shut. The nurse that has followed us is standing beside me.

“Has she responded to anything yet?”

“No,” she says compassionately and places her hand on my shoulder.

“Tell me.” I don’t need to explain my question to her.

“She hit her head when she was shot, causing her to have bilateral subdural hematomas in the head. The neurosurgeon did a craniotomy and put in a drain to remove the excess fluid to relieve pressure, but she is still not responding.”

“Oh, Cady,” I rasp. “I’m so sorry.” I can’t stop the flood of tears.

Jon wakes up. "What? Has something changed?" There is fear in his eyes.

"No change," Zade says through his own tears

"Jon, I'm so sorry that Cady got caught up in my life."

"Don't say that. Cady loves you. When she heard you were in danger, she didn't hesitate to go with Zade, and he couldn't stop her."

"I tried. She told me I would have to drug her to keep her from going."

His words make me cry harder. "Cady, I know you can hear me. Fight! Fight with everything you have. I love you, and I need you in my life." I lay my head on her arm. I faintly hear Zade and Jon talking. I lift my head. "I can't leave Cady. You have to go find Kyren for me and convince him to stay. Help him, talk some sense into him. Just, please, bring him back to me."

"Brogan, I don't want to leave you."

"I promise I will stay here and do whatever the nurse wants. Just please go find him."

The nurse lets me stay with Cady and Jon.

It's several hours before Zade walks back into the room. Kyren is not with him. I frantically look around him, hoping that at any moment Kyren will walk in behind him.

"He's gone, Brogan. I'm so sorry, but he is gone. His yacht is gone."

About the Author

Kelly Moore was raised in Mt. Dora, Florida, a true southern girl with a sarcastic wit. Gypsy traveling nurse by day and romantic author by night. Loves all things romantic with a little spice and humor. Loves two characters who over comes their pasts to fall in love and have a happy ending. Wife, mother, grandmother and dog lover. Travels the US in a fifth wheel making memories and making friends.

Make sure to pick up your copy of the next book in the series Pieced Together to find out what happens.

http://amzn.to/1mU6Y9p

Join my Newsletter to keep up with all the newest releases, freebies, and teasers.

https://my.sendinblue.com/users/subscribe/js_id/2p1of/id/1

Follow me on facebook http://on.fb.me/1P9G9V4
Website www.kellymooreauthor.com
Amazon http://amzn.to/1mU6Y9p
Goodreads http://bit.ly/1RkemHh
Bookbub http://bit.ly/2hF0BbS

Made in the USA
Middletown, DE
11 August 2022